Big Easy Evil

Heather Graham

Prologue
Demons

"Come to me!"

Casey Cormier wasn't frightened at first; she thought she'd imagined the words. She was busy; deeply involved in the advertising design she was working on for a local Christmas festival to be put on by one of the major toy companies. And while it had been great to have Gill Martin and Chrissy Monroe come by to ooh and ah over the decorations, it had taken a bite out of time.

She had a lot of work to do.

They were still in October, of course, but in truth, that meant they were late for December, and she had been given a rush job.

"Casey!"

She did hear her name. She looked up, perplexed. She was alone in the house.

Gill and Chrissy had left well over an hour ago. Sean had left about fifteen minutes later.

From happy little dancing reindeer on her computer screen, she studied the Halloween decorations around the house. A rubber skeleton danced down from the archway to the kitchen; the walls were covered with broomstick-riding witches, demon faces, and jack-o-lanterns. The door that led to the foyer was decorated with skeletal and ghostly creatures, spiders, and bloody hearts. The crowning glory of the inside decorations was the life-sized ghostly vampire standing by the coffee table in the middle of the room; the thing was an antique, "Mr. Devil Demon," one-half of a prize Sean had found at an auction for theme-park owners and operators.

"Mrs. Devil Demon" was outside, by the cemetery.

Casey was in the downstairs parlor of the Victorian house she knew so well—the New Orleans Garden District family home she was in the process of buying from her parents. Her mom and dad had moved down to Florida, anxious to spend their golden years out on their boat. Of course, what she paid them was nominal—enough to keep a pair of retirees going. And they were delighted she was there; the house had been in the family since it had been built back in 1855. It was home; she loved it. She was so comfortable here! She lived in the house now with Sean DeMille, the love of her life. They'd marry soon enough, when they could make all the right arrangements.

She shook her head, looking around. One of the Halloween pieces had to "talk." Motion activated or on a timer. It was a good thing she wasn't easily scared. Only the pieces right by her on the secretary were cheerful and leaning toward the fun side of Halloween; they were her purchases and one was a small, smiling jack-o-lantern made of papier-mâché or some such similar substance and the second was a metallic black kitty candle holder. She had also bought a poster of a silly, happy, dim-witted witch and that was up above the secretary on the wall.

Fun.

She had to concentrate. Cute little deer were in her world at the moment, while this...

Sean was the one who had gone a little bit Halloween crazy. The front yard had blow-up creatures—some from movies, some from popular lore, and it delighted Sean to no end watching dozens of people stop for pictures—some asking if they minded when they were home, and some hoping they weren't home when they opened the old iron gate to slip in for photo ops. His biggest thrill was bringing in the kids from the poorer districts—letting them shiver and laugh and...celebrate. But, Sean was also working for a living and his boss, Jeff Abernathy, had called. Ned Denton, the operating manager that night, couldn't solve a problem; and Sean, being Sean, had hurried in, certain he'd only be a few minutes.

And so, she was alone. Alone, and she'd been alone here dozens of times before. It was her home. She loved it. She was never afraid here...

But now...

"Casey..."

She heard her name called again. The sound was deep, husky, eerie...like something uttered from a long dead and dried out corpse.

And then she thought she heard a "No!"

As if there were two people in her house, one urging her to do something, and one urging her not to do something!

She stood, forgetting her computer—and the rush job for the moment.

A branch scraped against the side parlor window, making her scream and jump—and then feel like a fool.

It had been a branch—just a branch.

"*Casey...*"

"Sean, you're an ass!" she said aloud. That had to be the answer. Sean had set up something in the house, something motion-activated or on a timer. She adored Sean; they'd both grown up in New Orleans, but, Sean was three years older and been in a private school while she'd attended a public one; they hadn't met until they'd both been at LSU. His last year— her first. They were both in design, she more in art and graphics while his work had a great deal more to do with engineering.

Thus, the giant creatures in the front yard—and the "Cemetery Maze" he was setting up in the backyard, were all for the neighborhood children. Sean loved Halloween, and he loved what he did. Off time meant nothing—he was always working. He could be very serious, of course, but, he also had a playful and mischievous nature that could pop up often.

"Not funny—ass!" she said aloud.

There was no response.

She was going to kill him when he got home!

She glanced at her watch; he was hoping to be home by nine. He had gone to work out a few kinks at a local Halloween-horror themed attraction. While others in the company probably could have gone when a coffin was failing to pop open, Jeff had called Sean, so he had decided to go himself. He was in charge of the set-up; he would see to the problem.

Quarter of nine...

Maybe his timer had gone off a bit too soon. Sean had surely wanted to see her reaction to that eerie voice.

"Jerk!" she muttered. "Well, guess what, my boy? You are not going to scare me—you are not going to freak me out of my home!"

Determinedly, she sat back down at the old-fashioned secretary by the side window in the parlor. She made a point of looking at the poster of the smiling witch, and at the little black kitty that was really a candle holder, and then the dumb-looking jack-o-lantern right next to her computer.

Then, resolute, she looked back to the computer—and her work.

Cute little reindeer popped up on her screen.

The electricity suddenly went out and the room was pitched into darkness, only her computer screen setting off a glow.

And then she felt it; a touch on her shoulder.

The eerie, dry-leaf-rustle voice seemed to whisper in her ear again.

"Casey. Come to me."

"No, no, no, leave her!"

Two voices. In her head? Electronics, motion activated creatures, maybe, just maybe, she could have handled it.

But, with everything else, with the house plunged into darkness...

"Casey, no, no, no..."

And that was it. She let out a terrified scream and leapt up. She could have headed toward the foyer and the front door, but the back door seemed to be closer. She wasn't really thinking at all—she wanted out.

She had never been so terrified, so panicked, in her life.

Casey tore from the parlor and through the dark dining room to the large kitchen behind it, stumbling her way to the back door.

She found the bolt and slid it, pushed open the door and nearly fell back out onto the back porch. Neighborhood lights and a high-flying moon cast a pale, yellow glow over the back.

Sean's Halloween maze was halfway complete; a fiberglass recreation of cemetery gates rose high, surrounded by a broken fiberglass wall with skeletal parts stuck through the pretend bricks, as if they were parts of the dead trying to escape.

"Mrs. Devil Demon" stood at the gate—a wicked smile on her face—as she encouraged visitors to enter.

Casey felt a shove at her back.

A scream escaped her again, she went flying out to the entry to Sean's Halloween maze, through the "cemetery" gates, and past the sign, "Abandon all hope, ye who enter here!"

It was there she tripped.

At first, her mind was simply filled with blind terror—no logic registering at all. And then, she was trying to think. The moonlight and trickling of street lights served only to make it all the more...shadowed, and somehow...

Evil.

She could smell the dank earth, as if it were freshly dug. But, none of the graves back here was real, there were tombstones and mock-ups of the famous New Orleans vaults, "cities of the dead," and there were cherubs and angels and...

Something dark. A massive dark shadow that almost had shape...but, did not.

The black mass began to laugh and laugh...

The sound was like the rustling of dry leaves, yet somehow deep and throaty and...

Evil.

The word came to mind again.

Yes, as if evil had real shape and form, as if the concept itself was tangible.

She gasped, choking, even more terrified than before. And she tried to get to her feet; she had to rise and run out to the sidewalk, call neighbors, get help...

She rolled to push up.

For a moment, she thought she saw a flash of yellow light. Something that cut across the darkness.

She reached out to steady herself, trying to see, trying to understand...

And she touched something...strange.

Not quite cold. Not quite stiff. It had a feel of muscle and flesh beneath cloth...

One of Sean's props.

But, it wasn't, and she knew it.

The moon shifted; the black mass was gone. That light, too, was gone. That strange light...

And she was looking down at a dead man. A real one.

His face...his face had been bashed in by...oh, God, oh, God!

She screamed and screamed again.

Chapter 1

"Halloween! Thought to have originated with the Celtic holiday of Samhain. It was the golden time of fall, between the richness of the summer and the brutal cold of the coming winter. It was a time when great bonfires were lit to burn brilliantly to the heavens—and when people dressed in costumes, often fierce and terrifying, to ward off ghosts. And, Samhain was important, terribly important! Therefore, Pope Gregory III designated November 1st as All Saints Day— making the night before All Hallows Eve—and thus could he combine the custom of the people with the religion that was bit by bit conquering the countries of Europe. Since those early days, Halloween has evolved and been embraced with open arms by children—of all ages—greeting card agencies, and the makers and creators of all manner of rubber, plastic, cloth, and sometimes talking creatures, all for the delight and for a bit of a scare. Ah, and did I mention candy manufacturers?"

Shaking his head, Michael Quinn plopped down on the loveseat in the bedroom he shared with Danni Cafferty in the old French Quarter house on Royal Street serving both as their home and their curio/collectible/souvenir shop. He had been reading from a book he'd just purchased in the Garden District after meeting an old friend for lunch at Commander's Palace.

Danni, having just placed one of her favorite Halloween pieces, a benign and—in her words-- charmingly adorable and fluffy--stuffed cat in a witch's coned hat in the center of her dresser, leaned against the old mahogany piece of furniture, crossing her arms over her chest.

"Halloween," she informed him, "is supposed to be...well, as you said, it started out as a religious holiday, or a holiday to honor the dead. But, come on, people have made it into a...fun holiday. Kids love Halloween. You're very grim."

"In this city? Can't help it—Halloween and the days leading up to it? They make me just as uneasy as all hell."

"And that's because you look at every silly paper skeleton as if it's real."

"Because it damned well may be," Quinn said.

"Hey, let's not ruin a holiday for a city full of little kids, huh?" she asked.

"Just don't like it—don't like Halloween," he said.

"And that's okay."

"Yes, it is. But, I do always see..."

"Yes?"

"Whatever life brings, it's amazing. Because I have you."

"Oh, now, that is the—"

"Sweetest thing I could possibly say?"

Danni grinned. "Smartest," she told him.

He rose, walking over to her, slipping his arms around her. "Danni," he whispered softly, "sometimes, as we know, life can be just—good."

"Especially when I'm the smartest thing in your life, eh?"

"I was thinking..."

"Ah, yes, the most brilliant thing in your life," she teased.

He shook his head. "Right now, I was thinking..."

"Beyond brilliant?"

Again, he shook his head. "Sexy, provocative, enchanting...sensual, seductive..."

"Very good!" she teased,

"And we get to have fun. And enjoy the holidays, and one another. It's just, it's...Halloween."

For a moment, her eyes were on his, big and crystalline in their exquisite deep-blue color. He was always in love with her; deeply in love with her, but when she looked at him like that, heart, soul, mind, and body seemed to melt, even if--at first--he had thought of her only as Angus Cafferty's sadly naïve and spoiled daughter.

But, that had been long ago, and once Danni had accepted what her father had left her was far more than just a shop called *The Cheshire Cat*, she had sprung to the challenge with true fortitude and courage.

Because the shop—and the life—she had inherited were far more than a place where T-shirts, local crafts, and pieces of the past might be found and the day to day existence of a shopkeeper. In the basement, Angus Cafferty had collected and disarmed those things containing...evil. Angus had spent his life working to prevent what could really only be described as "possessed" and disarming them—and he had also spent his days protecting his artist daughter from the truth of what he did.

Angus never expected to die when he did. But then again, that was true with most men, and his death was now several years in the past.

"Hm," she murmured. "You're not so bad in that direction yourself, you know!"

Quinn slid his fingers from her shoulders down her back, and pulled her flush against him. She started to protest, and then she smiled and kissed him.

He was always in love. And far too easily aroused.

Holding her now, he was feeling his love and his arousal...

Knock, knock!

A little too passionately for the moment—since there was a knock at the bedroom door. Danni was an exquisite beauty with deep burnished auburn hair and a lithe build. Her eyes were brilliant, and compelling, but her smile was the best, and when her lips were on his...

The knock sounded again.

It was only two in the afternoon. The shop was open for business. There was no reason for anyone to suspect they might have grown amorous so early. Then again...

The knock came yet once again; hard and insistent this time.

"Quinn, Danni, ye be needed!"

It was Billie at the door. Billie McDougall. The man had come from Scotland years and years ago with Angus Cafferty, and he had served as Cafferty's right-hand man in all things.

And now, of course, he worked with Danni and Quinn.

"Later!" Danni whispered to Quinn, with a wicked pinch against his jeans.

Quinn gave her a, what he hoped was, a stern and yet equally wicked warning in return.

He walked over to the door and opened it.

Billie McDougall was one of the finest men he'd ever met—yet he could easily pass for an elderly Ichabod Crane, or perhaps "Riff-Raff" from an old-Broadway cast of "Rocky Horror."

"Someone needs to see you," he told Quinn.

Wolf—Quinn's massive wolfhound, roughly the size of a small horse, barked, as if in total agreement with Billie.

"The shop...?" Quinn asked.

"Shop is running just fine. Bo Ray has it all under control."

Bo Ray Tompkins had once been a "person of interest" in an investigation of Quinn's; he also suffered from addiction. Quinn had gotten Bo Ray beneath the wing of another friend—an amazing friend, Father Ryan—and, beneath him, Bo Ray had embraced life and sobriety—and become an amazing asset at the shop, and in their lives.

"It's busy; it's Halloween," Danni murmured.

"And Bo Ray has it all under control. But, I've got a man seated in the kitchen. You need to come now." He cast his steely blue-gray gaze over the two of them. "There's time for being a couple later, as ye well ought to know by now!"

Danni blushed and Quinn lowered his head, hiding a smile. "Hey, it's been quiet! We were enjoying being..."

"Marry one another, be getting it over with!" Billie commanded, shrugging as he turned away. "Not that it matters much these days, and not that the two of you are keeping two rooms, or whatever..." Billie muttered, walking away. "When I get to m'own great reward, old Angus will be sayin' to me, Billie McDougall! What we're ye thinking, not getting me lass up to the altar!"

He went on ahead of them. Danni and Quinn looked at one another, trying not to laugh.

"We do need to get married," Quinn said lightly.

He didn't wait for her response. She was still grinning. He headed after Billie, knowing she would follow.

As would Wolf. He was an amazing dog, completely loyal to Quinn, but well aware his true duty in life was to guard Danni now against all things, real and...shouldn't be real, but were!

In the kitchen, he found a young man. Blond, medium build, sitting at the table, nursing a cup of coffee. When the man saw Quinn and Danni enter, he leapt to his feet. His hair was long, falling over his forehead. His eyes were light and filled with anxiety.

"Michael Quinn, Danni Cafferty, this is Mr. Sean DeMille. He's in need of a private investigator. An open-minded private investigator."

Sean DeMille stepped forward to strenuously pump Quinn's hand, and then take Danni's and do the same.

"Please, sit back down, Mr. DeMille," Quinn said.

"Please. More coffee?" Danni asked, giving him one of her warm smiles. The man instantly seemed to ease a little; Danni had that kind of an effect on people.

He sat. "There was a murder," he began.

Quinn felt Danni's eyes on his. They'd both heard about it; a man named James Hornby had been killed the night before; it was a major news story. He'd been found in a Garden District yard, slashed to shreds as if a grizzly with buzz-saw teeth had gotten a hold of him—quite impossible in the city of New Orleans. The news had been focused on little other than the story that had broken just that morning.

If they hadn't already seen the news, Sean DeMille was ready to explain.

"He was ripped open—*ripped. Or hacked!* As if...as if some rabid creature with shark's teeth, or a were-creature tore him up," Sean DeMille said, shaking his head, still in disbelief. "An axe...my axe!...was sticking out of his head." He shook his head. "I don't know if...if the injuries killed him, or the axe. The axe would have killed him. I mean...it was in his head.

And I knew him!" he added softly. "Well, not as a friend, but I'd see him on Magazine Street, sitting against a shop wall or something...begging? I don't think he was a heroin addict or anything, just an old dude who had hit on hard times." He was thoughtful. "Jimmy! Yeah, his name was Jimmy." He looked at Michael Quinn with another sad shake of his head. "I didn't think of that—I didn't think of his name when the cops were there. But...Casey was just in such bad shape. She was convinced it was me. That I was the body. She was screaming and hysterical, and I was trying to calm her down, and it was so bad...and I don't know. I just don't know what the hell happened!"

"This occurred in your back yard?" Quinn asked.

Sean nodded. "I was working on it for Halloween...I love Halloween. I—I once loved Halloween. I do great decorations. Well, I create some of my own decorations, but mostly, I design sets or scenes or whatever...I design events for a living. Our front yard is fantastic. I love having the neighborhood kids in, or kids from anywhere. When I'm done, the day or so before Halloween, I have them bus in kids from other areas, kids who can't...can't pay to go to things. So, the house looks like a horror house, and the yard—front and back—looks like a theme park. But...I...we...don't own any animals. And I usually see Jimmy on Magazine Street. *Saw* Jimmy on Magazine Street. Poor Jimmy, poor Jimmy. It was...horrible."

"Go back a bit," Danni suggested softly. "Did you find the man? Or had Casey called the police?"

"I had been working on the new horror park in that old empty warehouse property in the CBD, Central Business District, you know? It's called *Horrible Hauntings.*"

"I know the place," Quinn said.

"I'm an engineer and designer," Sean said. "One of our coffins wasn't popping open when it should have been. I'm hands on—a lucky guy, I love my work. When there was a problem, I went in. Casey was working at the house. I still don't really understand what happened with her. She heard something. Someone pushed her. He called her name, and pushed her."

"Who called her name and pushed her?" Danni asked.

Sean shook his head, looking helpless. "There was no one in the house. And she thought she was hearing two voices. The police looked; they looked everywhere. I thought at first they were going to arrest Casey—or me!—except...there was no way she could have done such a thing. I mean, physically. I don't know how Jimmy came to be in the yard. I never had him to the house...I'd just give him money or buy him a meal sometimes. As far as I knew, he didn't have any idea of where I lived, and he wouldn't have considered me anyone special. I dialed 911 the second I arrived...there were a half dozen witnesses ready to swear to where I had been...and there was no blood on me or in the house, I mean. Or on Casey or me...and he'd been... ripped up, like I said. Ripped up by a...creature! The house belongs to Casey, really. She bought it from her parents. She grew up in that house! There's never been anything like this before...never. I've never seen anything like this before and I was...lord, I was in the military!"

"Where is Casey now?" Danni asked.

"Home. Exhausted. The forensic people and the police with them really just wrapped up about an hour ago."

"And Jimmy was found last night at about nine?" Danni asked.

"Yes, right about nine...and I think he hadn't been dead very long. The house has been searched and searched, and the yard, and Casey is exhausted, but, can't sleep." He shrugged suddenly. "I grew up here. It's not like I'm a good Catholic or a good anything, but when I go to church, it's Father Ryan's church, and I know he comes here a lot, and I always thought it was all hocus pocus, but...I know I need help! Casey's not alone. Gill and Chrissy are there...and my boss...feeling guilty, I guess. He had called me in. And the night manager, too. They're good people; they care, and they worry."

"But the police are all gone now, right?"

"There's just one cop, kind of watching over things in the back, I guess. He'll be there a while; the detective is coming back with some other expert. I needed to be there...but...I just...I just don't know where to go from here. We were up all night. We can't be afraid of our home, Casey loves it...and I need...I need to know what happened, where to go from here!"

Quinn looked at Danni. As he did so, his phone rang.

He glanced at his caller I.D.

It was Larue. Detective Jake Larue. Once upon a time—before Quinn had discovered his life was to be a bit different—he'd met Angus Cafferty and then Danni. And he'd learned just what the house on Royal Street housed, and every crime could come with a greater evil than even that which existed in the hearts of some men. That evil, though, often found men and women with whom it could easily attach.

"Excuse me," Quinn said. He stood up and walked back into the hall that connected the kitchen, Danni's studio, the stairs to the second floor—and the shop, *The Cheshire Cat.*

"I've got one for you," Larue said. "Need your help."

Larue didn't really understand quite what Quinn and Danni did. He just knew they could be really helpful in certain circumstances. He was a good cop; best detective Quinn had ever known.

But, Larue didn't really know exactly what they did. He didn't want to know.

"Dead man attacked in the Garden District?" Quinn asked. "Ripped up as if by a creature with razor-sharp teeth."

"You've heard."

"Couldn't really miss it. But, no real details. I just heard about a man being found on the news, and now...there's a man named Sean DeMille sitting in the kitchen right now."

"Yeah, well, I still have a cop in his back yard. Forensics spent the night going through the place. As far as we can tell, neither the killer nor the victim was ever in the house, but...we picked up some big patches of earth along with the body." He was quiet for a minute. "There was an axe left in the victim's head. The axe belonged to Sean DeMille; he used it in his work in the back yard."

"I heard."

"We don't know if the killer would have found another method to kill...if the axe happened to be there, or what. So much blood...anyway. Want to meet me in the Garden District? Or should I swing by for you?"

"Pick me up; I'll leave Danni the car. She can talk to Sean while we're still here and then...then do some research."

"Five minutes," Larue said.

"Should I bring Sean DeMille with me?"

"Hell, yes. He's the only one who is going to know what goes on and off in that yard of his!"

Quinn returned to the kitchen. Sean's hand was on the table; Danni's was gently laid over it.

Billie McDougall was leaning against the stove. He nodded to Quinn as he entered.

He'd stay here with Danni; he knew exactly where Quinn was going.

"Sean, I'm not sure how you knew to come to Danni and me," Quinn said, "but I used to be partnered up with the lead detective on the case. Can you come with me? Did you drive here?"

Sean shook his head. "I took the street car and then walked through the Quarter."

"All right, good." He looked at Danni.

Check the book, please?

Danni, of course, lowered her head in agreement, and then rose and looked at her visitor. "Anything you need, Sean, you just come on back here, okay?"

"Thank you!" the man said. "Thank you."

Wolf barked.

Quinn showed Sean the way out through the kitchen door to the courtyard. At the door, he looked at Danni.

See? He questioned silently. *Halloween! Wrong holiday, but...*

Bah! Humbug!

***

Stairs from the hallway led down to the basement and to what had been Angus Cafferty's office—and private collection.

Danni still didn't fully understand—and probably never would—just what caused certain objects to bring out murder and mayhem and pure horror.

She had adored her father. He'd been older when she'd been born, but the man had been a Highlander! Fierce, tall, broad-shouldered, and strong—and the kindest human being she had ever met, a gentle giant. A good human being. She had thought she'd have him forever.

And, of course, he had surely not intended to die when he did, leaving her to learn everything she needed to know about their "curios" and "collection" from Michael Quinn and Billie. And, naturally, since Quinn had known things about her father she hadn't, she had started off thinking of him as the biggest ass she'd ever met...

Amazing how that had changed! She thought of the way he had been so intent on his reading, and then the way he had held her, hazel eyes deeply intent and almost gold, a lock of sandy hair falling over his forehead.

She'd come to adore him; he was her lover, and her companion is so many ways. Quinn was a good six-foot four and every inch of that was solid, lean, muscle. She couldn't imagine trusting anyone more, or becoming involved with anyone else so completely and passionately.

She wondered if he'd known something had happened, someone would be coming to see them. Of course, they'd known about the murder, but...

It might have been something easily explained, drug related, accidental...

Larue didn't call on them unless there was something unusual.

And—before becoming amorous!—Quinn had seemed moody, as if he'd been waiting for something to happen. Maybe he did have a bit of a strange sixth sense. She had definitely learned all things were possible in the years since her father had died—and she'd met Quinn.

She heard a soft whine. Wolf.

The dog had followed her downstairs. Ever her guardian.

"Wolf, you know, Quinn and I really do need to get married. We keep saying it...and we keep getting involved in other things, and, well, you know! We have friends who want a big thing, but, hey, maybe Vegas! An elopement!"

Wolf let out an approving bark, wagging his tail.

Danni sat down at what she still referred to as "her father's desk," and picked up his book. It wasn't any book known in the world, like the "Book of the Dead," or any such thing. It was her father's book, but it had come down through their family, through a long line of...curio collectors. And within its pages were fonts of information, info on evil people through the ages, on the objects they had owned, on *things* that sometimes held onto the evil of those who had owned them—or even had them fashioned in order that their souls—if they could be called souls!—might live on. In the past, they had dealt with an evil bust, an evil painting, murders in the bayou...and more.

She sat down and began to carefully search through the pages of the book—ancient, she thought, though she doubted even her father had known how old it was.

Of course, she didn't even know what she was looking for.

"So, Wolf. Halloween came about because of the ancient Celtic holiday, Samhaim, Christianized into All Hallows Eve. And then, hm, there's a great story about the jack-o-lantern. Do you know that one, Wolf? The tradition started in Ireland, too, so they say. There was this fellow—named Jack, of course, who was always tricking people and dealing with them in a very shady way. Anyway, he didn't want to go to hell, so one day he trapped the devil in a tree—got him up that tree and pinned him there with crosses, because we all know, the devil can't cross a cross—and then made the devil swear he would never take him into hell. The devil swore—and Jack let him go. Well, then, just go figure! Jack dies, as all men must die, and when he gets up to Heaven, Saint Peter says Jack was way too badly behaved in life to enter Heaven. So, Jack tries to get into hell—but the devil is good to his word and refuses to let Jack in! Jack is therefore forced to roam the netherworld, the darkness, for eternity, and to light his way, he finds a turnip—there were no pumpkins back then in Ireland—and he lit up his turnip to guide him through the darkness and ward off evil spirits! What do you think of that, Wolf?"

Wolf dutifully barked, as if he'd been enthralled by her story.

"Remind me, Wolf, with all this going on—we're going to need a lot of lanterns."

She flipped more pages, wishing there was a computer search engine that could help her. She could just key in the words, "savage beasts that axe in heads and rip mortals to pieces."

But, she didn't have a search engine.

Billie stuck his head in the doorway.

"How's it going?" he asked her.

"Slow!" she told him. She looked at him.

"Keep at it," he said quietly. "We're fine; Bo Ray has the shop in good shape; it's busy as usual, but he can move like a bat out of hell, so all is well. And while you keep at it, I'll help him."

"Sure," she said. "I just...I need to go there, too, you know. I need to see where this happened; I need to see some of the things in Sean's display. I'm..."

She stopped.

She'd flipped a page.

And the page's headline read, "Savage beasts that axe in heads and rip mortals to pieces."

Chapter 2

Sean DeMille was a little awkward when Jake Larue pulled off on the side of the road in front of the shop to collect the two of them. Quinn realized Sean and Larue had naturally met the night before, when Larue had first been called out to the scene of the crime.

"Hello, sir," Sean said. "I just...well, it's so horrible I thought we could use any and all help and I know how busy the police are and—"

"It's okay, Mr. DeMille. As you can see, I called Quinn in on this, too," Larue said. He glanced at Quinn. Quinn grimaced. "Our crime scene people have been through the house and the yard, and we're good to go with all else."

"We should get going," Quinn suggested quietly.

"Hop in." Larue said.

Sean took the backseat; Quinn the front.

Larue was a good cop, a year or two older than Quinn's mid-thirties. He wasn't quite as tall; he was a lean man with the perfect manner for his job. He could be tough as nails, and also easy enough to encourage those who could help to do so. He told Quinn sometimes, at first sight, Quinn was more intimidating, being well over six feet and with some of the city remembering he had once been a golden boy in the city, a football hero who had thrilled many an armchair quarterback. But, Quinn had been horrible at being revered; too much, too soon—and he had flat lined because of an overdose of drugs and alcohol. And in that time...

Someone, something, had been there. A guardian angel? The force of his imagination? At any rate, he'd seen himself there, seen himself dying—and seen something or someone else. One way or another, he'd been given a second chance.

And he'd changed his life, being a cop...and then finding there was more in the world than met the average eye and then, of course, Angus Cafferty.

And Danni.

"I don't know what to do," Sean said bleakly from the back. "I had arrangements with some of the schools. Halloween week. They're supposed to be bringing the kids out...Wednesday, Thursday, and Friday. Wednesday. That's tomorrow. What will I do? I mean...even if the scene...even if you release the yard or whatever cops do, how can I bring kids to a yard where a man was mauled to death by...by something that doesn't exist?" he asked desperately. "Oh, lord, I'm horrible. I'm worried about what to do and a man was killed. It's just for some of the kids...it's a big deal. Something they look forward to because...because it's all they get."

"You're not horrible," Quinn said. "While we're still living, we still worry about what we do."

Sean nodded. "Not the yard...not the yard. What if I'd had a kid in there?"

"You didn't," Larue said.

"Change of venue," Quinn suggested. "Maybe you can still do something for the kids at another venue."

"We don't know another venue," Sean said bleakly. "Casey owns the house. We do okay, but, we're not rich."

"We might be able to find someone to help," Quinn said, glancing at Larue.

"You know someone?" Larue asked, frowning.

Quinn grinned. "We both know someone."

And they did. On one of their most peculiar cases, they'd become friends with one of the richest women in the city, Hattie Lamont. They had, in fact, wound up on a deadly mission to Switzerland regarding a deadly painting with Hattie, and since then, she'd been a wonderful, helpful part of a small group in the city who knew a great deal more about *The Cheshire Cat* than the rest of the populace.

They reached the house; the yard was gated and fenced, and Larue pulled up on the street.

Quinn got out of the car and surveyed the place.

Sean DeMille definitely loved Halloween.

"For the kids!" Sean whispered.

In the front, many of his decorations were blow-up creatures from literature, legend, and lore.

A very creepy headless horseman extended a hand toward the front door. Vampires and wolfmen hovered on either side, as if they were about to vie for the goods to be found inside the house. Movie monsters looked at the vampires and wolfmen—as if perplexed. Quinn could see the tableaus had been set with lights, and he imagined, at night, with those lights shining on the creatures, it could be very frightening, indeed. But, as if to assure the kids there was a bit of fun included, too, there was a friendly looking giant dinosaur overlooking it all.

"I don't like to scare the kids too much. I mean, the scares should be fun," Sean said.

He opened the gate to the house; Quinn noticed there were no locks on the gate. Sean obviously didn't care if people slipped in for fun or photo ops.

"Who is here?" Larue asked Sean.

He nodded. "Casey, and, of course, she's not alone. I—I don't know if she'll ever stay here alone again. Friends are here. Chrissy Monroe. She works with Casey at their graphics studio. Gill Martin, Chrissy's boyfriend, great guy. And my boss—Jeff Abernathy. Oh, yeah, and Ned Denton—he's the night manager. I think Jeff and Ned think...well, it wouldn't have been so hard on Casey if I'd been here. It wouldn't have happened! I'd be damned if I'd let anyone—real or imagined!—push her around or terrify her or..." His voice trailed and he stared bleakly ahead.

He led the way to the path taking them to the entry of the house, opened the doors, and brought them in.

The parlor of the old house was a wicked repeat of the front yard—without the friendly looking dinosaur. In the center of the room was a very real-looking vampire in the old tradition, white shirt, black tuxedo jacket and pants. It was a handsome vampire—except for the eerie smile and the barely showing fangs.

Did the thing come to life? Had it ripped up a human being?

He didn't have a chance to ask Sean about the vampire at first; there were two young women who rose from a sofa as they entered, one a petite redhead and the other a taller brunette.

There were three men in the room as well; one was forty-five or so, medium in height and build, with close-cropped graying hair. The man standing nearest the brunette was probably in his mid-thirties, tall, lean, and with a headful of long wild hair and large dark eyes. The way he stood, close to the brunette, led Quinn to believe they were together. The third man was tall and lean, anxious looking, with short brown hair he pushed nervously off his forehead, and, like the second man, somewhere in his mid to late thirties.

"Casey, I've brought Quinn," Sean said. "Quinn...that's Gill Martin," he said, indicating the long-haired man. "And my boss, Jeff Abernathy, and Ned Denton, night manager at the haunted house. Oh, and I'm sorry, Casey, of course, and Chrissy Monroe."

Casey was evidently the tiny redhead, as she stepped forward right away. Quinn reckoned she was in her early twenties—twenty-five, tops. The other woman appeared to be a few years older, possibly closer to thirty.

"Mr. Quinn, thank you for coming!" Casey said, and then she quickly looked guilty. "Detective Larue, I'm sorry. I mean, I have faith in our police..."

"It's all right. Quinn came with me," Larue said.

"Oh, oh, well...thank you," Casey said. She looked a little uncomfortable. She looked from Quinn to Larue. "I'm—I'm not being hysterical, you know. I'm not on any drugs; I'm steady and fine and in my right mind, or however you say it."

"Yes, I believe you," Larue said.

"We can't begin to understand what happened!" Gill Martin said, shaking his head. He glanced over at Casey and Chrissy. "We had been here...we'd come to visit...we'd just left maybe an hour before it seemed to have all...happened."

"I'm so sorry we left!" Chrissy said. "But, Casey needed to work."

"And, of course, I'm sorry as all hell I called Sean in," Abernathy offered.

"I should have dealt with the problem; it was no big deal," Denton added.

"What happened, happened," Casey said, "and it wasn't anybody's fault." Once again, she looked at Quinn. And then she burst out with, "There was something in here. Something, someone pulling strings. I heard my name. I *felt* a touch. I—I thought you might believe me. And it was...so strange. It was like there were two voices, one pushing at me, one pulling at me. And, I swear to you, I am not crazy."

"Casey, we believe you," Chrissy murmured uncomfortably.

"Maybe there *was* someone, something, in here—pulling strings," Quinn said gently. He looked at the others in the room. "So, Chrissy, Gill—you two were here?"

"Yes, we left at about eight. Oh, my God! Maybe the poor man was being murdered when we were here! Maybe we didn't hear anything when it was—happening," Chrissy said with horror.

"We were here—and we were drinking coffee," Gill offered. "We weren't plastered or anything. Only coffee. That was it."

"I was completely sober and in my right mind," Casey said softly.

"I'm sure you were," Quinn said. "Can you tell me what happened?" he asked Casey. "I know you've said it over and over, but..."

"No, no, I understand. You need to hear it all. Then you want to see the yard," Casey said dully. "Of course. I was there, at the old secretary. I was working on Christmas. I'm a designer. We're late for Christmas," she explained.

"Of course," Quinn said gently.

"Then, I heard it."

"It?" Quinn asked.

"A voice. Like rustling dry leaves. I thought it was one of Sean's silly decorations, on a timer or...motion activated. I don't know. Anyway...I heard it again. And then something touched me. And I should have run out front, but the back seemed closer...seemed to be away from the voice or the touch or whatever. I didn't see anything. I went out back."

Quinn paused, looking around at the decorations in the house. The vampire was life-sized. In Quinn's mind, Casey couldn't have been much of a scaredy-cat. Not if she was working with the vampire in the house.

Quinn walked up to the thing.

As he did so, Jeff Abernathy said, "A prize! A true prize. I've been trying to buy him and his mate off Sean, but..."

"A prize!" Sean offered, sounding bitter. "I bought him and his wife or partner or fellow vampire at an auction. It's old—dates way back. Maybe the turn of the century. She's out back—in the cemetery." He let out a long sigh. "Oh, God, little did I know it was really going to turn into a cemetery."

Quinn gave his attention to the piece. It had been created with a metal frame, he thought, and covered with a rubber-like substance. The clothing was made of fine cloth, and the artwork on the face was fantastic. The thing looked real.

Quinn stared at it.

It stared at Quinn.

But, it seemed benign. Absolutely benign.

He turned to Larue. "The back?" he asked.

"Excuse us," Larue said to Sean and the others.

Larue led the way out toward the arched doorway to the kitchen. Quinn paused again, looking back.

Sean DeMille did love Halloween. All kinds of creepy decorations had been set up. Bloody finger-prints, spiders, cauldrons, witches. Most were scary. A few—like the smiling and cheerful jack-o-lantern on the secretary—were more cheerful. One of the witch posters offered a truly happy, matronly looking witch with a friendly smile and a basket of candy.

There were dozens of things here, if not more than a hundred! If an object here was cursed or evil, it could take forever...

But Halloween was coming. And whether Danni wanted to think of it as candy and kids in charming costumes or not, it could bring about...

Bad things. Very bad things.

Like a man torn to shreds.

Casey and Sean were together, watching as Quinn headed out with Larue.

Behind them were Chrissy Monroe, Gill Martin, Jeff Abernathy, and the night manager at the horror house, Ned Denton.

Abernathy and Denton hadn't been at the house that night, or—at least they had not mentioned being there. Abernathy had called Sean in. And if Denton was the night manager, he'd been at the horror house.

Chrissy and Gill had been in the house—an hour before Casey had thought herself under attack. Before she had heard the voice, been pushed—and stumbled upon a dead man.

"I've talked to them, of course," Larue said, as they slipped out the back.

"And?"

"Sounds like they were all together for a bit of a social evening, and then Chrissy and Gill left—just as they said. I sure as hell can't prove otherwise. And as to Abernathy and Denton...well, Abernathy said he was at home. When there was a problem, Denton called Abernathy and Abernathy called Sean, and he went on in—leaving Casey alone. I wish to hell I could point to a person. Quinn, I had people crawling all over this place last night—cops going door to door to find out if anyone had seen or heard anyone. Techs trying to find any kind of a clue. They searched the house up and down. No forced entry. We don't know what the hell drove Casey outside. Her imagination? It can play tricks, you know."

"Yes, the imagination can play tricks," Quinn agreed.

"Here; the marker is still there. That's where we found the body."

Quinn could see where the body had lain, clearly marked by the police.

He wished he had been here the night before, that he had seen it all before the police had come through.

He believed in the cops and in Larue—he had been a cop.

But now, there was little left to see. Just the marker. The shape of the body.

He moved around, noting the decorations, the "cemetery" gates, the signs...

"Blood?" he asked.

"On the victim...we picked up bits and pieces of decoration with blood. Even dirt."

"Were there animals around? Any sign of animals?"

"No, this is how we have it—Sean DeMille came home right after Casey Cormier fell on the body. She was hysterical. She couldn't see the victim's face. Oh, by the way, it was easy enough to discover his identity; the man—James Hornby, known to most as Jimmy--was a Vietnamese War veteran, fallen upon hard times. He remained cheerful and helpful while accepting handouts on Magazine Street, most of the time. How he came to be here, we don't know. He was lured here, and killed here. What we can't figure, of course, is the way he's ripped up—along with the axe in the head. The axe, as I said, was here—Sean had been splitting up wood for the creation of his cemetery here."

"And you suspected neither of them?"

"DeMille called 911 as soon as he got here; neither of them was covered in the kind of blood you'd expect they'd be covered in. And Casey was hysterical. We checked, of course, on Sean DeMille. He had literally just left his place of employment, and the techs checked Casey's computer—her last entries were just seconds before she came outside."

Quinn nodded. He didn't believe either of the pair he had just met could be guilty of this. Then again, you never knew. But, when time factors were involved, they were pretty solid as far as proving innocence.

"The body was here...and this thing was here?" Quinn asked. He was referring to a life-sized vampire figure that appeared to be the mate to the one inside. The mannequin or life-sized doll was beautiful; it had long dark hair, a refined face, and huge, haunting eyes.

The two mannequins or life-sized dolls were so very real—and compelling. The clothing was just a little ragged—as if they were old. He couldn't help but wonder if there was something about the two of them, or one of them, or...

Any one of another of the Halloween decorations that were set up about the house.

Or maybe there was nothing at all. Maybe someone with a rabid dog, perhaps suffering from rabies themselves, had come upon the man...

Quinn turned to Larue.

"The autopsy was scheduled for today?"

Around the country, whether a state went by a medical examiner's office or a coroner, a body was usually brought in and—unless there were impossible circumstances—given an autopsy the next day.

Larue nodded.

"I'd like to accompany you to the autopsy."

"Of course," Larue said. He glanced at his watch. "Hey, I didn't call you because I *wasn't* looking for help on this damned thing."

Quinn nodded. "Thanks. This is..."

"Halloween—and still, weird as shit. I mean, yes, we have bad things happen. Wackos seem to like to come to New Orleans to do horrible things for Halloween. But, this...Anyway. We have thirty minutes or so before leaving, if you want to look around."

Of course, Quinn wanted to keep looking around.

He just wished to hell he knew what he was looking for.

Quinn looked toward the house. There were six people in the house, each of them involved in one way or another.

The answers might lie out here somewhere.

Or...

They might well lie inside.

He went to stare at "Mrs. Devil Demon."

He closed his eyes, and then he looked at her again. She was really a beautiful piece. And while wicked, her smile and eyes seemed to be teasing...

Was she sweetly teasing?

Or was there something in that smile that was deadly?

***

Danni read, both fascinated and repelled by what she discovered under the very specific heading she'd been so stunned to discover.

"Evil...defined by devils or demons, perhaps cursed souls bringing their wrath upon innocent humanity.

In 1942, while America was engaged in World War II, a young woman came to the police with a fantastic story. Her husband, out of boot camp and given a weekend before deployment to Europe, was savagely murdered and left lying in the bayou. She said there was an axe or hatchet protruding from his skull; his body had been ripped and mauled, as if by a savage beast.

The police returned to the scene with her; they found blood, but no sign whatsoever of the body.

The husband, however, was never seen again; the young wife was arrested but quickly released for lack of evidence. Some assumed the wildlife in the bayou—a hungry gator, perhaps—took off with the body. Others assumed the wife had killed him, and made the body disappear so it could never be used as evidence against her.

In the 1950s, while going through records, Detective Stan Garfield, researching cold cases, discovered every record of the event had disappeared.

In 1972, a tourist was found murdered—an axe in his head, limbs torn to shreds—near Saint Louis #1. A frantic local ran to the church to call for help. When the police came, there was no body. In the days to come, it was discovered Barry Alexander of Clinton, Mississippi, had headed for New Orleans, never to be seen again.

In 1980, Eric Garfield—a detective, like his father—again picked up the cold case. He, too, discovered the records were missing.

Evil exists, and evil lives, and evil finds roots in those who have the hearts and souls to encourage and nurture its growth.

Between May 1918 through October 1919, twelve people were known to have been attacked by an assailant who came to be known as the Axeman of New Orleans. The Axeman was never discovered, never caught, never brought to justice, though there were many suspects. Records from the time, however were sketchy, and neither Garfield, father nor son, had ever been able to discover any connection between the Axeman assaults of 1918-19, and the later disappearance/murders."

Danni sat back, looking at the book and frowning. Every kid in New Orleans knew about the Axeman. A Jazz song had been written about him. His exploits—dramatically, of course—were told around campfires and at slumber parties, and she'd even heard a well-told tale aboard a "haunted bayou" trip.

That much was known as fact—there had been an "Axeman" busy in the New Orleans area. He could be found in many books about unsolved crimes. At the time, forensics hadn't been able to make discoveries due to DNA and other more modern techniques.

He had usually used an axe—found at the place where he assaulted people. Of the twelve attacked, if she remembered correctly, five had survived. And one of the survivors had even become a suspect.

She started reading again.

"The evil in men can live on through memory, and through belief in evil powers; equally, it can be stopped when the soul through which it lives believes the power is gone. As in the others, so in the Axeman. For the soul believes in the power of the dead; what is deceased must be brought back to powerlessness. Evil is often brought back through the remnants of he who held the last weapon, he who believed he could control the elements and creatures of the earth. Destroy that which has been brought back, and destroy the evil."

Wolf whined and came to sit by her feet. Danni patted his head and absently stared at the book.

She flipped the page.

There was no more.

"'Destroy that which has been brought back, and destroy the evil,'" Danni said aloud. "Okay, Wolf, what is the evil that has been brought back?"

She closed the book and stood up. She needed to know more about the Axeman of New Orleans—and who might have followed in his footsteps.

But...

"Wolf, what about the 'beast' aspect of this? Where did the beast come into it?"

Her cell phone rang and she glanced down at it quickly. Quinn.

She answered. "Hey, anything?" she asked.

"I'm going to autopsy. Danni, this place is filled with...things. Vampire mannequins, giant spiders, skeletons...anyway, I'm going to autopsy with Larue. I want to find out if Jimmy was killed by the axe and then ripped up, or..."

"I hope it was the first."

"Did you find anything?"

"I think so. Quinn, what do you know about the Axeman of New Orleans?"

"He killed a lot of people and was never discovered. Oh, he wrote a letter to the paper—or, at least, it's assumed the killer was the one who wrote the letter. He talked about killing—and about the belief he'd never be caught. He never was caught." Quinn was silent a minute. "He was active in 1920, or something like that. Danni, he can't still be alive."

"There were some other strange murders after. And there was a detective team, or a father and a son, really, trying to discover what happened in other murders that occurred decades later—one of them in 1972."

"What were the names of the detectives?" he asked.

"Garfield."

"Garfield?"

"Yes."

"I know a Garfield. Eric Garfield. He retired when I was with the NYPD. He was a good guy; his son became a cop, too, I think, but not here, not in NOLA. I'm not sure where he went, but...Danni, look him up. I think he still lives in NOLA somewhere. Danni, you have to be careful; maybe you should meet me at the morgue. You can wait in reception."

"I think I should find retired policeman Garfield," she said.

"Danni—"

"The other murders were decades ago. And according to dad's book, there was only one murder each time. Or, at least, that anyone knew about. I'll be all right; I have wolf. I'll keep in close touch; I promise!"

She hung up before he could argue.

Her laptop was upstairs; she quickly headed out of the basement—which was really just about street level, steps led upward to entries to the house, to the shop and to the kitchen door—and headed for her studio where she kept her easel, another desk, and all her art supplies.

And where, when she could, she worked.

And where sometimes...

She sketched or painted. And when she did, interesting things appeared on canvas.

"First things first, Wolf," she told the dog.

She sat at the desk there and flipped open her computer and looked up Eric Garfield, grateful for the Internet. Of course, not everyone popped up on the Internet, but...

Stan Garfield, retired detective, NOPD, was on social media. She found his page. He was now a grandfather; pictures of children and puppies littered his feed.

She flipped out of the social network—she could message him, but that would take too long.

She was thrilled to discover he had a phone number that was listed!

She dialed the man, her fingers shaking.

When he answered, she quickly dove in. "Hi, Detective Garfield, you don't know me, but, I was hoping you'd give me a few minutes—"

"Not detective anymore, miss. I'm retired."

"Yes, sir, I know, but I need to speak to you about some old cases and some research you were doing—"

"Who is this?" he demanded.

"My name is Danni—Danielle—Cafferty. I know this is going to sound ridiculous, but—"

"Cafferty?"

"Yes, sir."

There was a long pause.

"You're Angus's kid?"

"Yes, sir."

She heard a long sigh from the other end.

"I knew your father," he said quietly.

She wondered if that was good—or bad.

But, he then asked. "When do you want to meet?"

"Now?" she suggested. "Anywhere you like."

"Here," he told her wearily. "I heard about the murder in the Garden District. You can come on over. Come on over now. I'm in Treme, not far from St. Louis #1 and Our Lady of Guadalupe Chapel." He gave her an exact address and she thanked him and then remembered her promise to Quinn.

"Sir, do you like big dogs?"

"Love them. Bring your dog; come on over."

Chapter 3

Larue had connections and abilities in New Orleans.

Quinn was glad to see he'd arranged for Dr. Ron Hubert to perform the autopsy on James Hornby.

Hubert had gone through his own traumatic situation when a painting done by one of his ancestors had appeared in New Orleans; he had worked with Quinn and Danni and their crew before.

He wasn't surprised to see Quinn.

He was halfway through the autopsy when they arrived, and greeted them both with a nod.

"Larue, Quinn," he said. "As you can see...we're about halfway through here. And, while such a thing as this can never be happy, as far as our victim goes...there's a bit of good news. He didn't suffer long. The blow to his head caused an immediate blackout and nearly instant death. The other injuries you see here occurred post mortem."

And they could see the injuries, certainly. The man's arm had been nearly ripped from his body. Bite marks were all over the body.

"What caused the injuries—the bites?" Larue asked.

"Different creatures, as you can see by the differences in the size and the damage. I'd say you had a few dogs on him, and—I have some testing to do, of course—but it also appears as if he was attacked by squirrels and birds."

"Squirrels?" Quinn said.

Hubert shrugged. "That's what I believe at this moment."

"And...birds?" Larue asked.

"Vultures, kites, hawks...more testing," Hubert told them.

Larue looked at Quinn.

"That's...we believed he was killed right before he was found. Do you have a better time of death?"

"I was there last night," Hubert reminded him. "I was off—I'd just poured a brandy in my living room and was setting in for a nice night of reading when you called. And I told you then he'd been killed very recently—perhaps an hour and a half before I got there at nine-fifteen. Perhaps less."

"Then how the hell did those beasts have time to get at him?"

"Larue, you're the detective," Hubert said.

"And how did they all disappear so quickly?" Quinn wondered aloud.

Hubert looked at him. He didn't speak out loud, but Quinn knew what he was thinking.

You're the guy who figures out what strange and evil things are going on!

"Quinn, damn, you know I—of all people!—will be happy to help in any way I can. But, how animals got a hold of this man so quickly, I do not know. Oh, I believe he was killed on site. How he got there, I don't know. But, I've gone through blood loss and taken into consideration what was done to the body, and I believe he walked right into that backyard Halloween cemetery, got an axe in the head, died—and was chewed. As to the nature of the beasts..." He broke off and shrugged.

"Do we have an infestation of rabid squirrels in the city?" Larue asked, frowning. "If so—"

"Nope. Squirrels aren't rabid. We've tested some of the saliva," Hubert said. "Hey," he added quietly. "I'm on this, I've pulled in every favor with every lab tech out there. I promise you—I'll be doing my part."

Quinn knew Hubert would do as he said.

"Anything else?" Larue asked.

Hubert nodded. "Believe it or not, it might have been merciful. Mr. Hornby was suffering from cancer of the pancreas. He might have gone through hell before he died."

"Small mercy," Quinn noted.

They learned a few other facts.

James Hornby had been six-two, one hundred and ninety pounds. He'd suffered shrapnel wounds when he'd been in the service.

He'd had somewhere between three months and six months left to live.

They thanked Hubert and stepped back into the bright Louisiana sunshine.

Larue looked at Quinn.

"What the hell? Squirrels? Birds?"

"At least it wasn't a grizzly," Quinn said. "Or a single beast. Beasts...were involved. A pack of animals descended upon him."

"Vultures...that, at least, makes sense. But squirrels?"

"None of it really makes sense," Quinn said.

"No. And what scares me most..."

"Is it might happen again," Quinn said grimly.

"What do you suggest?"

"The same thing you would suggest," Quinn said.

"Interview the squirrels?" Larue asked dryly.

"If only we could. No. Interview every person in close contact with—"

"The victim--James Hornby?"

"You take that on. I want to know more about Casey Cormier and Sean DeMille—their friends, and the people at that event company where Sean works. Curious he was called out when he was, don't you think?"

***

Eric Garfield's place wasn't far, just across Rampart Street.

Danni truly loved her city. All of it. While *The Cheshire Cat* was in the French Quarter, or Vieux Carre, Treme was not far. Canal Street and Esplanade were boundaries for the Quarter, and the Mississippi River and Rampart Street completed what was more or less the oblong box that made up the section.

She could walk across Rampart and reach Eric Garfield, and she chose to do so.

All of the city, so it seemed, had gone a bit crazy for Halloween. Decorations were everywhere. Mannequins of movie monsters, literary horrors, and more stood sentinel in front of shop after shop. In many of the more residential areas beyond Bourbon Street, she saw that locals had gone just as wild with all manner of creatures and creations.

At one time, she thought she should have driven; Wolf was truly an amazing big dog, a wolf hybrid in truth, and many people stopped and stared, some frightened, and many others just captivated—and anxious to ask if they could pet him.

Wolf just took it all in—as if adoration was his due and he was entirely ready to be patient and accept all the attention.

She finally reached Rampart and she found herself looking at *Our Lady of Guadalupe Chapel,* the beautiful old structure once known as the *Chapel of Saint Anthony of Padua*. It had been built in 1826 as the burial chapel for the many dying of yellow fever in NOLA—from the chapel, they could be brought straight over to St. Louis #1 for interment.

The church was beautiful, and while it was still an amazing place and an active church—Danni absolutely loved the jazz mass there—there was something haunting and sad about it as well. And, of course, St. Louis #1 had the same haunting and sad feelings. Not to mention St. Louis #2, and St. Louis #3. The cemeteries were beautiful; they were truly "cities of the dead." And still, in their decaying splendor, they whispered of lives lost, often far too soon.

Danni and Wolf crossed Rampart and skirted around the church she loved so much.

Treme was a great neighborhood. Of course, TV had embraced it, and there had been times when it had been known for drug deals and crime. But it was also where many carriage companies kept their mules and many wonderful and fascinating people lived as well.

She glanced at her phone for the address Garfield had given her. She and Wolf had come to his house; a little one-story shotgun house, just in from Rampart. There was a white picket fence with a gate, and the gate easily swung open. There was a porch up several steps, indicating that a basement—really just the first level of the place—existed beneath the main structure.

Like the fence, it was painted white.

Eric Garfield had made one concession to Halloween—a blow-up cartoon character in an orange costume and holding a big bowl of candy was dead center on the left section of the yard.

The porch door opened and Eric Garfield stepped out as she swung open the gate. He waited for her and Wolf as she approached the porch.

He appeared to be just about sixty or so. He had a fine head of almost pure white hair, a lean face that seemed aged by both frown and smile lines, and a tall, lean, still hard-muscled body structure.

"Beautiful dog," he told her. "And friendly, of course."

She smiled. "Unless you attack me, he is a sweetie. Say hello, Wolf."

Wolf woofed out a greeting.

"And you're Danni. Danni Cafferty."

"Yes, sir."

"Come on it. You, too, Wolf."

She entered the little house.

"Office, my room, whatever, this side," Eric Garfield said, indicating a doorway to her right from the entry.

Danni and Wolf headed into the room.

It was an amazing place. It was a library, an office—it had a comfortable couch at one end, and a large-screen TV. It also had a desk, piled high with papers.

The walls were also covered with papers—articles, posters, pictures, and more. Some were on corkboard attached to the walls; some were just taped straight on to the wall itself.

"Wow!" she murmured.

"Wow is good," he told her. "Some people walk in and think, hmm, this guy is sick as hell. But, I guess I am my dad...he passed away about six years ago."

"I'm sorry."

"He was ninety—he had a good life. And he gave me one, too. But, yes, like him, I can be damned obsessive. So, anyway, I believe I know where you're going. I—like anyone who had on a TV or computer or any form of media in the city and beyond—have heard about the murder. And I'd be curious about how the hell you heard about me—except I did know your father." He was silent for a minute, looking at her. "And, I've heard rumors you're continuing his work, and Michael Quinn is working with you, right?"

"Yes," Danni said simply.

Eric sighed softly. "I've been chasing this—like my dad—for a lifetime. Don't get me wrong; I've lived a good life. I was a good cop—solved a lot of bad shit. But, this...there's something out there. Well, there may be many things out there. But on this...what you're looking for may well start with that clipping right there. Oh, it's not original—it's a copy. I may look old, but, I wasn't around in 1919 myself. Neither was my dad. Many detectives and armchair sleuths have that letter—or copies of it. And there are lots of theories, some better than others. But, officially, the Axeman of New Orleans was never caught. That, though, is supposedly a copy of a real letter he sent to the *Times-Picayune*. You've heard of the Axeman of New Orleans, right?"

"Of course. I grew up here," Danni said. "I need some refreshers on the events, though. I know many people believe the killings might have been mob related—many or most of the victims were Italian, right?"

"Yes. The first couple killed were Joseph Maggio and his wife, Catherine. They were grocers, and they were killed in their apartment over their grocery store. Their throats were slashed and then their heads were bashed in with an axe—both weapons found at the site. Oh, and the killer left his bloody clothes behind. That wouldn't have been such a good idea today, but, back then..." His voice trailed and he shrugged. "A month or so later, Louis Besumer and his mistress, Harriet Lowe, were attacked. They survived after the attack, and the papers went wild—but, most people were concerned with the scandal of the mistress bit. Oh, Besumer was a grocer. And Harriett had to have surgery—she died after the surgery, but before she died, she said she suspected

Besumer had done it. I've never been sure how to figure that fact with Besumer, who had a massive crack in his head—not the kind you give yourself. Besumer was arrested and imprisoned for nine months, but he was acquitted in May of 1919. Next," Eric continued, "was a twenty-eight-year-old pregnant woman, Mrs. Edward Schneider. She was brutally attacked—but lived to have her baby. Five days later another grocer was attacked—Joseph Romano. His nieces saw the attacker escape, but they couldn't identify him. He was described as dark-skinned, which could have meant African, Italian, Spanish...I'm not sure. Romano survived to get to the hospital, but then died."

"Did the nieces say anything else?" Danni asked.

"They said the assailant wore a dark suit and a dark slouched hat," Eric told her, walking closer and leaning against the wall, his arms crossed over his chest.

"I remember there was a song written about the Axeman. A jazz song," Danni said.

"Indeed. *The Mysterious Axeman's Jazz, Don't Scare Me, Pap.* It was written by Joseph John Davilla. Local publishers."

"And the rest of the victims?" Danni asked. "I can't really see the Italian mob being after a group of grocers."

"Maybe they weren't paying protection," Eric suggested.

"Maybe the Axeman had a vendetta for having purchased spoiled veggies," Danni murmured. "I mean, he went after a pregnant woman, too. Hard to tell how he figured his attacks. Who were the next victims?"

"Charles, Rosie, and Mary Cortimiglia. They were over in Gretna, across the bridge. Two-year-old Mary was killed in her mother's arms. Charles and Mary survived; she accused neighbors, a father and son. An old man too feeble to have come through the panel the attacker used—and the son way too big. They went to prison, but Mary recanted—she had accused them out of bitterness, so it seemed—and the two were released. Charles and Mary divorced."

"They lost a two-year-old child," Danni murmured. "They were brutally attacked. Who knows what was going on in the woman's mind?"

"Steve Boca, Sarah Laumann, and Mike Pepitone," Eric said, and Danni knew he had studied the attacks backwards and forwards, and didn't need to refer to notes. "They were the last attacked by the infamous Axeman. Boca recovered and Laumann recovered. They couldn't identify their attacker. Pepitone died; his wife saw his attacker fleeing, but, she saw only a large, dark figure. She was left with six children. And the letter—the copy you see on the wall here—was sent in between the Cortimiglia murders and the attack on Boca. Go ahead. Read it."

He waited. Danni walked closer to the wall and read.

"Hell, March 13

Esteemed Mortal:

They have never caught me and they never will. They have never seen me, for I am invisible, even as the ether that surrounds your earth. I am not a human being, but a spirit and a demon from the hottest hell. I am what you Orleanians and your foolish police call the Axeman.

When I see fit, I shall come and claim other victims. I alone know whom they shall be. I shall leave no clue except my bloody axe, besmeared with blood and brains of he whom I have sent below to keep me company.

If you wish you may tell the police to be careful not to rile me. Of course, I am a reasonable spirit. I take no offense at the way they have conducted their investigations in the past. In fact, they have been so utterly stupid as to not only amuse me, but His Satanic Majesty, Francis Josef, etc. But tell them to beware. Let them not try to discover what I am, for it were better that they were never born than to incur the wrath of the Axeman. I don't think there is any need of such a warning, for I feel sure the police will always dodge me, as they have in the past. They are wise and know how to keep away from all harm.

Undoubtedly, you Orleanians think of me as a most horrible murderer, which I am, but I could be much worse if I wanted to. If I wished, I could pay a visit to your city every night. At will I could slay thousands of your best citizens, for I am in close relationship with the Angel of Death.

Now, to be exact, at 12:15 (earthly time) on next Tuesday night [March 19, 1919], I am going to pass over New Orleans.

In my infinite mercy, I am going to make a little proposition to you people. Here it is:

I am very fond of jazz music, and I swear by all the devils in the nether regions that every person shall be spared in whose home a jazz band is in full swing at the time I have just mentioned. If everyone has a jazz band going, well, then, so much the better for you people. One thing is certain and that is that some of your people who do not jazz it on Tuesday night (if there be any) will get the axe.

Well, as I am cold and crave the warmth of my native Tartarus, and it is about time I leave your earthly home, I will cease my discourse. Hoping that thou wilt publish this, that it may go well with thee, I have been, am and will be the worst spirit that ever existed either in fact or realm of fancy.

The Axeman

"Do you think the letter was really from the Axeman?" Danni asked.

"I actually do. The fellow sounds sick as all hell. Nothing was ever stolen. And there were many Italians in the city, but I don't believe there was a mob connection. Everything was ransacked when the killer could, he left behind bloody clothing...I think that..."

He paused.

"Yes?" Danni said softly.

"I think that, like his letter suggests, he was just evil. Whether related to the damned devil or not, he was just evil."

She looked at him. "I read about later murders you and your dad investigated."

He nodded. "Murders—attacks—committed ala the Axeman. Maybe committed by a descendent? Most scholars and crime writers—and even fiction writers—seem to think the murders were committed by a man named Momfre or Monfre or some configuration of the name. It's possible he did have descendants and those descendants..."

"Descendants what?"

Eric shrugged, as if very careful about what he was going to say. "Maybe a man's descendants can inherit his evil. And maybe...lord knows, I don't! Maybe he sold his soul to the damned devil, or some such thing. That, of course, is not an official statement."

"Evil exists," Danni said softly. She kept her hand on Wolf's head; Eric seemed like a very decent man.

But there were papers and posters and articles referring to gruesome murders everywhere.

She was safe, of course. She had Wolf. And this man just might have answers or, at the least, clues to give them.

"Where did the 'beasts' come into it all?" she asked, aware her voice was barely a whisper.

"Ah!" His eyes brightened. "That's an aspect my dad investigated and, in a way—a very strange way—he might have found an answer." He hesitated again. "Truth is what we believe to be true—almost the same as...well, something really being true. Anyway, my dad did find something."

"Please!" Danni said softly.

He was still a minute. Then he said, "You are Angus's daughter. You won't think I'm...crazy."

"No, sir, I will not," Danni said.

He took another minute.

"Very well, then. I'll show you what my father found."

Chapter 4

Quinn had Larue drop him at Danni's house on Royal Street so he could pick up the car. He also wanted to check in with Billie and Danni—if she was there. He doubted she was. He had learned he couldn't shadow Danni as if he were an over-protective hen, but, then again—he loved her. That made it hard. He had friends that were couples also, who were cops, or both with the FBI—and they made it.

And he knew he and Danni would, too.

Though he couldn't control his feelings, he could control his actions.

He went through the front of the house, the business entry, into the shop—*The Cheshire Cat.* Bo Ray Tompkins was there, just as he should have been, weaving between customers. Clean and sober, he was a cheerful looking young man with a quick smile and easy way. He was great with their clientele, which, at the moment, was booming.

After all, it was Halloween week. The place was packed.

Bo Ray nodded to him and grinned; all was good.

Of course, it was. Angus had kept a good shop, and so did Danni. She was an excellent buyer—and she kept the shop intriguing, if not quite as intriguing as the basement!

She was a fine artist herself and sold a lot of her own sketches and paintings—and artwork by friends in the local community as well. She also found the most unusual and fun and/or interesting pieces of jewelry, clothing, and other knickknacks. The place was decorated with a number of antique pieces—benign pieces—and reproduction pieces that were high end and ever-changing when someone wanted to purchase something so unusual. But Danni was never in a hurry to sell the pieces, and while awaiting the right buyer, they gave the shop its character, and those included a Victorian coffin—filled with fun and unusual pendants, bracelets, and more. An Egyptian sarcophagus stood near the counter, and in October, it was kept slightly open, had shelves inside, and offered little pumpkins and other such paraphernalia.

Bo Ray left people admiring one of Danni's pieces—a charming oil painting of a black cat with huge gold eyes sitting in a field of flowers—and came to him.

"All is well here?" Quinn asked him.

"All going well. Danni will be happy—she bought some cute little semi-precious jewelry pieces from a local artist and they're going like hotcakes. Oh, and someone stopped by with some little pumpkins they want us to take on. Told them I had to wait for the owner on that. But, in here, all is well. Crazy good business during Halloween."

"Great," Quinn said. "Billie here? Danni?"

"Danni and Wolf left on foot. Billie just went down the street for a minute—to see Natasha." He glanced around the shop and then looked at Quinn and lowered his voice and said, "The murder in the Garden District, huh?"

"Yes. Nothing unusual has gone on here, right?"

Bo Ray shook his head. "Not that I know about, but…Billie wanted to see if Natasha had anything to offer on the subject."

"Thanks," Quinn told him. "If anything—"

"I'll call you right away."

Quinn nodded and headed through the door marked "Employees Only" and through the hall that led to the stairways, the studio, and the kitchen and to the courtyard and garage. They had a good thing going here; the house was one of the few to survive the fires that had ravaged New Orleans in 1788 and 1794, and it was very old and very well constructed—and beautiful. Billie McDougall and Bo Ray had their apartments up in the attic; he and Danni had the second floor for their personal space, and there was also room for guests when need be.

He paused, glancing into Danni's studio. He'd never quite figured out just what talent it was—perhaps it was even the power of suggestion. But, Danni sometimes "sleep-painted." And those paintings often offered them an insight into what was going on. He walked in and glanced at her easel. On the canvas, she was working on a witch standing in the middle of a pumpkin patch. A pretty witch, young, with a sweet smile, and dazzling little glitter-like sparks falling from her fingers.

He left the studio and headed on out to the courtyard, the garage, and the car.

Before hopping in, he called Danni.

She answered immediately.

He made himself speak casually. "How's it going?"

"I may be on to something; Eric is great."

"Always a good cop; tell him I say hello."

"I think you're going to need to see him yourself," Danni told him.

"Okay, I want to stop by *Horrible Hauntings,* and then check on Sean and Casey...and maybe get a minute to see friends of theirs—a couple. Chrissy Monroe and Gill Martin. The two had been at the house right before Casey stumbled on the body. Anything you want to tell me?"

"Yes, there's something all right, but...I'm still going through it all with Eric. Want to meet me here when you're done?"

"Sure... where?"

She gave him the address. He committed it to memory.

"Danni."

"Yes."

"Be careful."

"You, too."

They ended the call.

It was now early evening; the streets were growing busy. Some people were in costume, some were not, and many were already carrying the plastic containers that held the special drinks advertised by so many of the clubs and bars.

He chaffed; it took time to get out of the French Quarter.

He headed to the CBD, anxious to get to *Horrible Hauntings*, see what was there, and have a bit of a chat with the night manager, Ned Denton.

The old warehouse in the CBD wasn't far; it had long been rented out as a venue for parties, and this year, the building had been open as a Halloween haunted house since early mid-September. Quinn had heard it was good. Jeff Abernathy apparently paid his workers well, from those in construction and design to those working as "scare actors" in the venue. Still...

By the time he parked the car, it was getting dark. He was good at maneuvering the streets of New Orleans—the city had been his home, he'd been born and bred here.

But, Halloween was crazy. And parking was a nightmare.

He'd meant to just buy a ticket and go on in and survey the place a bit himself, but, even on a Tuesday night, the lines wrapped around the back. He found a security guard and introduced himself; the guard, like the rest of the city, had heard about the murders. He introduced himself as an investigator and friend, and the security guard slipped him on in through one of the employee entrances.

Like most such venues, the "horror rooms" were backed by dimly lit hallways for workers and security to utilize; they walked along one such hallway and came to a door that opened into a well-lit, make-shift office. There was a bank of screens there showing the various areas of the haunted venue, along with a desk, computer, and chairs.

Ned Denton was seated behind the desk.

He rose, surprised, but not dismayed, when he saw Quinn.

"Mr. Quinn, hello. How can I help you?" he asked.

"Sorry to bother," Quinn said.

"Not at all. I spend most of my time watching those screens—there's an asshole in every crowd. Some jerk who thinks it will be fun to mess with the actors and show off for his friends, or scare a girlfriend into a panic or some such thing. And, of course, just check the robotronics and all are working. Sit...and excuse me. I will be paying attention. Just watching the screens as well."

"Thank you." Quinn took a chair. He glanced at the screens. There were twelve of them; twelve themed areas were connected by hallways. For the most part, people seemed to be following along the route through it all just fine. Actors emerged from designated spots to pop up and scare people; motion-activated mannequins and more popped up as people walked by. People, startled, screamed delightedly. Some laughed uneasily. Some moved slowly—some hurried through.

"What can I do for you?" Denton asked.

"I was trying to find out if anything strange has gone on here at all."

Denton leaned back, letting out a long sigh "Strange, strange as hell what happened at Casey's and Sean's place. I know I saw Jimmy now and then...saw him on Magazine Street. I went over this afternoon when Sean called me—he didn't want Casey alone and he knew I'd be off during the day." He hesitated. "Of course, the body was gone, but, I never went outside. Everything I know, I know from what Casey and Sean told me."

"Sure. Anything strange happening here, though?"

"Besides the coffin in our autopsy room not popping open?" Denton asked.

"Anything at all that makes you worry...about an employee, an object..."

"An object?"

"Something might have been sabotaged in any way," Quinn said.

"Oh. No." Denton was quiet a minute. "Except for that coffin. It was working perfectly when we opened. Oh, we open at seven; I'm usually here by six. I was a little late today...you know. Sean and Casey...anyway, I guess that was it. The coffin. But, sometimes, anything mechanical can go whacky. But..."

"Can I see the coffin?" Quinn asked him.

"Now?"

"I know the place is busy, and, I'm sorry, but..."

Denton frowned. "You think someone might have purposely rigged the coffin so we'd call Sean in to work and..." His voice trailed.

"We eliminate everything," Quinn said.

Denton nodded. "Just let me call one of the security guys. Uh—there will be people in the room. Could you throw on a worker's executioner cloak and look like you're just...I don't know, checking out the condemned or something?"

"Sure," Quinn told him.

"I'll just get someone else in here," Denton said.

He picked up his phone and made a quick call; a security officer came in and Denton thanked him. He opened a cabinet door and came out with two cloaks.

He donned one and gave Quinn the other. They looked like medieval knight capes, and they were easy to slip on.

Quinn wasn't much in a costume mood, but...

They walked along one of the dark back hallways that had nothing but auxiliary lighting. Then they came to a makeshift doorway. Denton opened it and they slipped in.

The room was set up as if they were in a castle courtyard; false, aged brick lined the area, and there was a scaffold with a dummy and a slew of waiting coffins. An actor—an executioner—stood atop the scaffold, inviting visitors to come up to his "block," which, of course, was covered in stage blood.

He wielded an axe.

"Rubber!" Denton assured him in a whisper.

People were passing through. The actor was teasing and taunting them.

"Ah, fear not, I've help!" he said, "there will be executioners a-plenty, should my arm tire! You there—you! I can see you're guilty of the greatest heresy! Come, come!"

A girl screamed, and hurried on by—followed by her grinning boyfriend.

"There," Denton told Quinn.

He pointed to a plain and simple coffin—the type that might be used for a heretic or a traitor sometime back in history.

"See to it!" Quinn announced. "See to the executioners, for the coffin will be waiting!"

He walked to the coffin. As he did so, the lid popped open. A decaying corpse sat up.

"There! There lies the destiny of all traitors and heretics!" he proclaimed.

That got him to the coffin. The visitors paused to watch his bit of play--which was not what he intended. Under these circumstances, it was difficult to test the mechanism. But, kneeling down by the little ledge on which it was placed, he could see there was a sensor—it had opened when he'd come near. He looked at the latches and the sensor and noted there was still a bit of fluff—fluff from one of the very cloaks he was wearing—stuck to one of the latches.

He didn't have gloves or an evidence bag. That wouldn't have mattered; the cloak here might have been worn by dozens of people and touched by dozens more. He simply took the fluff—and slid it beneath his cloak and into his pocket.

He stood quickly and roared out, "There lies your fate!"

He headed back for the door by which he had entered. Ned Denton followed him.

"Hey, you're great!" Denton told him. "If you ever feel like you'd want to be a scare actor for a bit, please, let us know!" he said, leading the way back to the office.

When they reached it, he paused, shaking his head and frowning. "Sorry, did that help you any?"

"Maybe, maybe not. But, thank you. For your time, and for allowing me such easy access."

"No problem. It all seems so strange right now. Doing this...scaring people. When last night...a man was really murdered." He shuddered slightly. "Anything I can do, please, just let me know."

Quinn thanked him.

When he reached the car, he was glad he was headed up to a residential area—where throngs of people weren't oblivious to automobiles and it was easy enough to actually just drive.

He was anxious to see Danni—and anxious to discover what Eric Garfield might have to tell them.

But, first, he had to take a ride and see Sean DeMille.

***

"1942. Her name was Gretchen Amory. She was arrested after she came to the police station and claimed she needed help. Her husband had been murdered. The police went out to the site where she claimed she'd seen his body—and it was gone. The husband, Nathan Amory, was a soldier. He never reported back to base; he was going to be deployed. Now, many people believed the man was just a coward—and disappeared so as not to have to go to war. But, if so, his wife surely never knew anything about it. She raised her children and lived to the ripe old age of seventy without ever seeing her husband again, and she swore he'd been murdered in the swamp," Eric told Danni.

She was seated at his desk then, going through paper files.

"I—I heard about that," she said. "And I'm assuming it was easy for people to believe the man chose to disappear. Or, he was murdered by someone in the swamp, and either they or a gator came to get rid of the body. She was arrested though, right?"

"She was arrested, but let go the same day. There was no body. The police thought the husband had left her on purpose—or fled his military duty and probably the country. Thing is, I found something else. There was another murder at about the same time—over in Algiers. This one was...well, actually, it happened right before Nathan Amory disappeared. The body wasn't found for...a long time. Anyway, it was a Gordon Hampton; he was found in an abandoned bar—when neighbors finally noted the odor emanating from the property. He'd been dead weeks before the police got to him, and the medical examiner put it down to 'accidental death.' Apparently the corpse was so mutilated and chewed up—rats—they couldn't tell much. But! I found a diary entry written by a morgue assistant at the time. Gordon Hampton had been an itinerant, homeless, and frankly, no one had cared a lot. I can show you the diary entry; the dead man, according to him, was barely afforded the most basic autopsy. The injuries to his skull were chalked up to a fall. The morgue assistant was convinced the man had been murdered, but he also wanted to keep his job. He kept his thoughts quiet."

"So, there might have been an Axeman busy in the forties, too," Danni murmured.

"We had just gone to war—men were heading off to battle. Dying. People were struggling to exist; women were entering the workforce. I guess no one wanted to worry about a man it seemed life had already forgotten." Eric Garfield hesitated, smoothing his hair back. "I've found a few other incidents in that year. A knifing—chalked up to a bar brawl—in Gretna. Except there were no witnesses, and no arrests. And no one seems to have known who was brawling. Body was found by the dump in the back of the bar the next day when the manager came in—chewed badly by predators."

Danni was thoughtful. "There were no attacks on the body in the Axeman murders," she said. "What would...what would cause animals, big and small, to rip bodies to shreds?"

He shrugged. "Therein lies a mystery. But..."

He was quiet a minute.

"Let's move on to 1972. Barry Alexander—or the missing corpse we assume to be Barry Alexander. He was found by a tourist right in the heart of the city—right by St. Louis #1. When the police arrived on the site, there was no body. Okay, same year, not far away, up by Lake Pontchartrain—Belinda Montgomery found her father in the barn, a hatchet in his head. His body had been almost consumed by rats—overnight. Belinda was arrested, but let go. She hadn't been home the night before, and there were dozens of witnesses to swear to it. Another man, in Slidell, throat slashed, axe in his head— people believed he'd been the victim of a cult. The cult members did one of those cyanide things themselves, so there were no arrests and people then assumed the cult members had also come into NOLA and killed Barry Alexander as well. Maybe they used his body for some kind of rite."

Danni studied his face. "You don't think a cult did any of this."

He shook his head. "Crazy, right? I think it goes back to the New Orleans Axeman. Hell, I don't know if I believe in Satan, but...the letter the Axeman wrote...if anyone was being helped out by Satan, or some form of evil, it was him. My dad wondered if the Axeman might have been living somewhere else after 1920, and then come back here in 1942. But, if he'd been as young as twenty in 1920, by 1972 he'd have been seventy-two years old. And now...he'd be well over a hundred. So, logically, it can't be the Axeman who was attacking people in 1918-1919. But what if..."

Danni rose and walked over to read the Axeman's letter on the wall once again.

She read aloud, "*They have never caught me and they never will. They have never seen me, for I am invisible, even as the ether that surrounds your earth. I am not a human being, but a spirit and a demon from the hottest hell. I am what you Orleanians and your foolish police call the Axeman.*"

She looked back at Eric Garfield. "You think there's something to those words, don't you?"

He shrugged. "I don't know. Hell, I was a cop. I know people can be evil. But, can they leave evil behind? And if so, how do other people find it? Do axes just implant themselves in people's heads? And—while not with the original Axeman, but with the murders since, animals have torn the bodies to shreds. Rats in a barn, sure. But, corpses disappearing? I thought I could help you—with this other info. The thing is, I don't have any answers. I just don't know. Is this just all a set of bizarre circumstances? Was a cult active? Are there even any answers?"

"There are always answers," Danni said softly. "We just have to find them."

She'd been going to stay; she'd been going to wait for Quinn. But, she knew she needed to move on now; no telling what else might happen if they didn't get somewhere quickly.

She stood, and Wolf, who had curled up on the floor, stood as well.

"Thank you! Thank you. I'll be back with Quinn, if you don't mind. He'll need to see all this."

"I don't mind at all. I'd like some answers. The kind that will let me play with my grandkids. And Quinn...well, I remember when he was the talk of the town. And when he almost died—and then turned it all around. He was a rookie when I retired. But, you could tell he was going to be a good cop. Too bad he left the force, but then...well, he found your dad. And this pup, here, huh? Guess he's right where he's supposed to be."

Danni smiled. "And with me," she said softly.

She thanked Eric again, and then she headed out, back toward her own block on Royal Street. Her very good friend was there.

In her own shop.

Natasha LaRouche ran a voodoo shop. Her customers were tourists, of course.

And locals.

She was a priestess, a woman who took her religion very seriously. She read palms and tea leaves and people. She believed in goodness and all the right things.

One of her best friends was Father Ryan—a Catholic priest, and friends with Quinn before Danni had met Quinn herself.

Between them...

They were both very good at reading people. Natasha read cards and tea leaves; Father Ryan was extremely fond of reading the New Testament.

Between them, they were excellent at ferreting out and reading...

Evil.

Chapter 5

When he reached the home in the Garden District where Sean DeMille and Casey Cormier were living, Quinn found Sean in the front yard—taking down his decorations.

"Hey. Sorry...tearing all this down. No way in hell I want kids coming around here this year, not after...what happened. Hate it. I'm going to have to call the schools and tell them I have nothing for the kids."

"Don't do that yet; I can call a friend," Sean said.

"With a big yard? Who is willing to let me put up all this kind of stuff?"

"With a big yard, and a big heart," Quinn said.

"Well, thanks. Anyway, let me know." He sounded appreciative, but not as if he believed anything good could happen.

"Have you...gotten anywhere?" Sean asked anxiously.

"I went by *Horrible Hauntings,*" Quinn told him. "I saw the coffin you were called in to fix. What did you find to be the problem?"

Sean looked perplexed. He paused in his work, wiping his brow. He didn't seem defensive, just confused.

"Did something happen there?" he asked worriedly.

"No, no. When you went in to work, what was wrong with the coffin?"

"Some idiot closed it on one of those cape things they use when they need to enter in where people are being scared. It caught in the mechanism. Easiest fix ever. But...it took me away from Casey. And I'm...man, I'm still worried about her. This is slower than it needs to be—I keep going inside to make sure she's all right. Oh, and I took that stupid vampire thing out back with the other one—think I'm going to burn the pair."

Burning something that might be evil, or associated with evil, or even tainted with evil might not be a bad thing.

Then again, if the mannequins were benign and it was something else...

"Don't do anything to them. Not now," Quinn said.

"I want them out of here, away from here, so badly!" Sean said.

"I'll take them with me. And if you want them back later, you can have them. But, I'd like to work on this a little longer, okay?"

"I just wish that...well, come in. Casey is trying to work. She sits for a minute, and then jumps up, and comes out here. Unless I go in there, she forgets what she's doing and comes out here."

"Any way you guys could get away for a few days?" Quinn asked.

Sean gave him a weary look. "You said you went to *Horrible Hauntings*. The place is filled with electronic devices that can go awry. We both do okay. We just can't afford to lose our jobs."

"What about a hotel room?" Quinn asked.

Sean laughed. "Have you ever tried to book a room in New Orleans at Halloween?"

"Okay, I see your point."

Maybe they shouldn't be at the house. They could stay in a guest room at the house on Royal Street, but, he'd have to check with Danni first.

"Anyway, come on in, please," Sean said.

Quinn followed him into the house. There had been an amazing transformation.

The place had been cleared out of anything that even slightly resembled Halloween.

"Where is Mr. Devil Demon?" Quinn said quietly to Sean.

"Outside, in the back, with Mrs. Devil Demon," Sean told him. "I told you...I want to burn them! And everything else that was in here and in the yard...."

Casey was sitting at a secretary; her computer was there.

Her desk was bare.

Even the cute little poster that had been above the secretary was gone.

"Mr. Quinn!" Casey said. She stood quickly and walked over to him, looking at him anxiously. "Did you find out anything—anything at all?"

"I don't know anything, except…" he hesitated. Casey was both frightened, and deeply pained that a man had been killed. "The medical examiner said Jimmy—the man killed in the yard—died just about instantly when the axe hit him. He didn't feel…anything else. Also, he had cancer. He wouldn't have had long to live."

Casey studied him, and she smiled grimly. "Small favors!" she whispered. "And the medical examiner was telling the truth?"

"I know the man well. He wouldn't lie."

"Well, that's good. But…"

"He went to *Horrible Hauntings,*" Sean told her.

"Oh?"

"Casey, let's sit, shall we?" Quinn asked.

"Okay," she said slowly, her voice tremulous. "Did something else…"

"Let's sit."

They sat. Then Casey leapt up off the sofa. "What's the matter with me?! Mr. Quinn, would you like some iced tea, lemonade—or a beer?"

"Casey, I'm fine, and it's just 'Quinn.' Everyone just calls me Quinn."

"Okay," she said, glancing at Sean.

"I need you to think, to really think about all the things that were in here—and the people who were here, too. And, if you've come across anyone—anyone at all—who might have wanted to scare you, or even do something bad to you."

Her eyes became enormous. Sean was sitting next to her and she clasped his hand. "Me?" she said, her voice a little squeak. "But…they killed James Hornby!"

"And you were lured out of the house," he said.

"Maybe you were imagining things," Sean said. "Halloween is...suggestive. Not in crazy way—not in a crazy way at all. But, I may have gotten too carried away."

"Way too carried away, Sean DeMille!" she said.

"Casey," Quinn said, trying to get her to focus. "I need to know. And, Sean, what about you? Is anyone jealous of you at work? Do you have any enemies?"

"Me? Enemies...no. I'm a hard worker. Honest. And I didn't steal anyone else's job," Sean said. He shook his head. "There's no reason for anyone to want to hurt me."

"Or me!" Casey said

"And it was...it was Jimmy who was killed," Sean said.

"I understand, but I think someone purposely made the coffin top stick. I found a piece of fluff in it...and you said it had been stuck because of a cloak. Who has access to those cloaks?"

"Well, anyone working security. In fact, anyone working. Mr. Abernathy, Ned, the actors, the workers...the cloaks are kept in the office. Employees wear them when they have to go in to check on something when the attraction is open."

"And Abernathy likes you—doesn't resent you?"

"Of course not. I'm really good."

"What about Ned?"

"He loves me!" Sean said. "As an employee. We've gotten fairly close as friends."

"Did you know Abernathy and Ned Denton before you took on the job?" Quinn asked.

"I've worked several attractions as Abernathy's employee. I work holidays, events for kids. And for retirees. Mainly holidays. You know, Easter attractions, Christmas, New Years."

"What about Ned Denton?"

"Same thing. He's been around as long as I have...about three years."

"And your friends?" Quinn asked.

"Chrissy and Gill?" Casey asked. "Chrissy and I both work for *Paper People*. We're artists, graphic designers, and we work with paper engineers. Cards and books and things like that."

"For how long?"

"Same thing...not quite so long. Two years, maybe. Chrissy is one of the nicest people I know. What are you getting at? Our friends wouldn't want to hurt us! And, oh, God, they'd never, never put an axe in a man's head!" Casey said. She looked at Quinn, horrified. The she looked at Sean. "I thought you said he found out...why weird things happened. Evil things."

"He does—hey! Father Ryan said he was the man to see!" Sean protested.

"Casey, please don't get angry with Sean—or with me," Quinn said. "I have to ask these questions." He couldn't let up—he felt it was urgent they move fast.

Before someone else wound up with an axe in their head.

"What about Gill Martin?" he asked.

"He...he's nice. Chrissy loves him," Casey said defensively.

"They haven't been dating long," Sean said. "But, he seems to be a great guy. He works for one of the construction companies as an electrician. It was really nice of the two of them to come by today along with Jeff Abernathy and Ned. They took time from work. They...they're friends."

"All right, thank you," Quinn said. "One more thing— Casey, you heard two voices?"

"No one believes I heard even one," she said bitterly. She looked at him, stubborn defiance in her eyes then. "Yes. I heard two voices. One said to come...the other to stay."

"All right," Quinn said. "I'll be back with you later."

"Tonight?" Casey asked anxiously.

"Tonight," he promised. "If I have anything—if I don't have anything. I'll be back with you."

He started for the door. Sean jumped up behind him. "Wait!"

Quinn paused. "Yes."

"You said you'd take them—Mr. and Mrs. Devil Demon. You said you'd get them out of here."

"Okay. We'll get them in the back of the SUV," Quinn said.

"Oh, thank you!" Casey said, clasping her hands together as she stood.

Sean walked over to join him at the door.

"Come on; I'll help you get the suckers out of here!"

Quinn accompanied Sean out back. The yard had been torn apart. Some of the decorations still lay on the ground—dismantled and ready to be taken away.

Mr. and Mrs. Devil Demon now stood together, right beneath the cemetery sign that read, "Abandon all hope, ye who enter here!"

"Turned out to be true for old Jimmy," Sean said sadly. He looked at Quinn. "What the hell was the man doing here, do you think?"

"I don't know," Quinn told him. "Larue has been working on that all day."

He picked up Mr. Devil Demon. The thing only weighed about thirty pounds.

Sean had Mrs. Devil Demon. The two of them walked to his car and manipulated the pieces into the back.

Quinn stared at them for a moment before closing the hatch.

Nothing. He didn't feel anything evil or ill about the pair at all.

But, what else...

Evil—in human form?

Had someone purposely lured Sean from his home that night?

He couldn't help but believe it was so.

And yet...

It was getting late. He was anxious to find out what Danni had learned from Eric Garfield.

He was, in fact, anxious to see the man again himself.

**

Natasha LaRouche, or, Madame LaBelle—her professional name—was one of the most fascinating women Danni had ever known. She was regal, beautiful, and fit her "la belle" very well. Tall, lean, with skin the color of café au lait and striking features, she was ageless.

While she made a nice income reading tarot cards, palms, and tea leaves, her shop was her life's blood. She kept an incredible shop filled with books on history—especially the real history of voodoo. It was Hollywood who had turned the religion into something wicked, she often said. That, of course, and Papa Doc Duvalier, the despot dictator who had ruled Haiti so long.

She was beloved, and her kindness and wisdom would have worked well in any religion; she preached kindness to one's fellow, care for the aging and handicapped, and love for all children. People came to her with their problems.

And in all things, and in any possible way she could, she helped Danni and Quinn.

The shop was crazy when Danni arrived with Wolf; she didn't go in, but rather headed straight to the courtyard where Natasha often met customers. She had a covered table out there with a beautiful crystal ball.

With the crowd inside, Danni didn't want to try to maneuver the herbs and talismans and all else on the shelves with Wolf—and his massive tail.

Natasha, of course, loved Wolf. He would have been welcome. But, Danni went into the courtyard. Natasha wasn't there, but Jez, her tall, equally impressive assistant, was gathering up tea cups.

"Danni, hey. Wickedly nuts, huh? Halloween. You wouldn't believe the people coming in here who think we sell 'voodoo' costumes!"

"I'd believe just about anything," Danni told him. "I know how busy you are, but do you think I could speak with Natasha for just a minute?"

Jez looked at her a moment and set a tea cup back down.

"Sure. She thought you might be coming. The murder, right? The poor old man axed in a Garden District yard?"

Danni nodded.

"Yeah, I thought it was weird enough for Cafferty and Quinn. Hang on. I'll get her."

He went in. Within seconds, Natasha was hurrying on out. She was as beautiful and exotic as ever, wearing a colorful headdress and a caftan in shades of orange and aqua.

"Danni!" She greeted her with a hug, and then turned to dote on Wolf. "Thought you might be coming by. How awful...and frightening. People are talking about haunted houses, costumes—and the murder. Sit down, sit down."

"You're so busy now!"

"It's okay. I have extra clerks working. And, this...well, this takes precedence. Sit, sit, tell me what you know."

Danni sat. Wolf perched between her and Natasha.

Danni told her about the day, from the time Sean had come in, until she'd seen Eric Garfield.

"Natasha...this isn't happening every twenty years, but twenty or so years seem to go by before these murders and or disappearances take place. I can't help but wonder...if the evil is something? Sean DeMille went crazy with decorations. I haven't seen them, but I've heard him talk about his Halloween, and I've heard a bit from Quinn."

"We both know evil can latch to objects, and yet, those objects will usually latch on to the evil in a man or woman," Natasha said. "What about these people—Casey and Sean?"

"Sean seemed sincere," Danni said. "And, apparently, Casey was terrified. Absolutely terrified. Something was after her—in her house, or so she believed. Oh! And our mutual friend, Father Ryan, told Sean he should look up Quinn."

"We should call our mutual friend," Natasha said. "I'm sure—even if he told Sean to go to Quinn—he's already been looking into things himself."

"Has anyone come into your shop hoping for something you *don't* sell?"

"Black magic?" Natasha asked. "An evil voodoo spell?" She sighed. "We get a lot of people who want love spells, and sometimes, of course, we have people who want to jinx a neighbor or a boss or someone. I don't think I've ever had anyone ask outright for a spell that would make a *thing* or another person kill someone."

"Of course not," Danni said. "But, if someone was strange..."

"Strange. In a voodoo shop. In New Orleans,"

"Natasha!"

"I know, I know, I know what you mean! I'm trying to remember. Let me call Jez back out here and see if he met anyone strange."

"Asked for...strange herbs or potions or spells."

Natasha smiled. "I know exactly what you mean, not to worry!"

She rose and headed back for the shop.

Danni patted Wolf's head. "If you ask me, Wolf, it's all...strange, at the least!"

Her phone rang. She saw the caller I.D. and answered quickly. It was Quinn.

"Hey!"

"I thought you were waiting for me at Eric Garfield's house," he said.

"Oh! I'm sorry. I talked to him. I thought I should speak with Natasha. I was trying to move as quickly as possible."

"Where are you?"

"Natasha's. I'm fine. I have Wolf."

"I'll meet you there."

"I have so much to tell you—"

"I know. I've just left Eric's house; I've seen what you've seen. And...I think we have something of a direction to go in. I'll be there soon. I'm almost there."

"Great," she murmured. "See you soon."

Natasha was coming back out of the shop with Jez

She wasn't smiling anymore. She looked disturbed and grim.

"Jez, tell Danni about the woman who came in—asking how to wake the dead."

Jez looked from Natasha to Danni. "I did have a woman in here last week asking about voodoo spells. I explained that to us, voodoo was our religion, our tenets were about goodness, and we didn't do any kind of evil spells. She said, oh, she wasn't being evil, she just wanted to reach out to someone in her past. She wanted to wake the dead. In spirit, in her mind, of course."

"What did she look like?" Danni asked.

"Medusa."

"Be serious, please."

"I am being serious. She was dressed up in a great Medusa costume. Snakes coming out of her head and all. It was a fabulous costume."

"Was she white, black, Asian...?"

"Green."

"Pardon?"

"I don't know whether she was white, black, Native American, Indian—or Asian," Jez said. "She was wearing paint and probably prosthetics, too. I'm sorry, Danni. But—because we do get a lot of the very strange in here—I honestly remember her because her damned costume was so good."

"It isn't even Halloween yet!" Danni said.

"I know, but, there are parties going on all over town."

"You're right, you're right, and, I'm sorry. And it might not mean anything at all anyway, Jez. Thank you!"

Wolf barked; Danni saw Quinn was walking into the courtyard.

Danni stood, anxious to see him. He walked up to the table where Jez and Natasha had grouped around Danni.

"Okay, Quinn is here! I think that means, repeat it all again!" Jez said.

"Whatever it is, please!" Quinn said. He swept out a hand. Natasha and Jez took seats at the table, too, and Quinn sat then, too, setting a hand on Wolf's head.

He listened as Jez repeated his story, and then he looked at Danni.

"What are you thinking?"

"I don't know—exactly. But these murders take place every few decades. And I was thinking maybe the Axeman had—descendants."

"And if he did," Natasha said. "They might want to carry out his work."

"It's not a bizarre idea," Danni said.

"Not at all. It occurred to me, too." He took a breath. "I was at Sean's work; I think the coffin failed to open—at *Horrible Hauntings*," he explained, for the benefit of Natasha and Jez, "was rigged. Someone wanted him away from the house."

"But," Danni said, "there was no one in the house—and Casey heard voices."

"And," Natasha said, "Someone was here, trying to find spells to wake the dead."

"Maybe just a party-goer," Jez said. "Crazy people think we'll give them weird voodoo spells all the time."

"But, we need a theory," Quinn said. "So...the Axeman has a descendant, or, at the least, a follower. An admirer. That person wanted to reach out to him—and, whoever he was, he's definitely dead. That person rigged the coffin, making Sean leave the house. And..."

"The voices," Danni said.

"The voices," Quinn agreed.

"We've seen objects before...that hold the evil essence of someone. So, this person found a way to bring the essence of a killer to life. How?"

"A spell to raise the dead or the spirit of the dead or..." Jez's voice trailed.

"The Axeman claimed he was Satan, of a demon or associate of the devil—he claimed he wasn't human," Danni said. "In his letter to the paper."

"The New Orleans Axeman?" Jez said. He shuddered. "I'll be playing jazz music tonight! Remember-he wrote he was going to kill on a certain date unless there was jazz everywhere. I heard every home had some kind of jazz playing."

"We'll all listen to jazz!" Danni said.

"Tonight," Quinn said wearily. "Tomorrow, we'll get together. We'll get Father Ryan out here, too. If I know him, he's been looking things up all day. And, I'm sure if we don't call him, he'll be calling us."

"I'll send out feelers—see if anyone else knows anything about people wanting to wake the dead or speak to lost souls," Natasha said.

Quinn rose and reached for Danni's hand. "I have a question for you," he said.

"Shoot."

"I'd like to ask Casey and Sean to stay with us."

"You're—you're sure you're not worried about the two of them having any involvement?"

"As sure as it's possible to be. I think someone around them did this...maybe it was a tease, before coming right after them. Killing them," he added softly.

"Bring them in," Danni said.

"I already have Mr. and Mrs. Devil Demon," Quinn said.

"What?"

"A couple of the decorations. They were bought at an auction, I believe. They're really great antique pieces."

"Mr. and Mrs. Devil Demon. Great. Hell, we might as well ask the Axeman in himself."

Maybe they already had!

But then again...

Weren't they the ones who were supposed to fight him?

Danni smiled at Natasha and Jez. "Well, I guess I'm going to go and meet the Devils," she said.

"Quinn, are you sure about what you're doing?" Natasha asked worriedly.

"I just have a strange feeling," he said. "I have a feeling that...well, I think these devils may be a force for good. Go figure. Anyway...Halloween is soon...really soon. And I'm afraid if we don't get this thing figured out..."

"All Hallows Eve will turn into the night of the bloody dead," Natasha said. "Jez and I will both be here through the night; you know to call!"

Danni, Quinn, and Wolf bid them goodbye and headed out of the courtyard and back out to Royal Street.

"You're sure you're okay with this?" Quinn asked Danni.

She smiled. "We'll get the guest room set up. We don't need both guest rooms, do we? I mean, Mr. and Mrs. Devil Demon don't need a room, do they?"

He shook his head.

"They'll look great in the shop. They're in the car; I'll get Billie to help me bring them in."

"Can't wait!"

Thirty minutes later, Danni had made the call to invite Casey and Sean to their house; she was afraid Sean was going to cry, he seemed so grateful.

And Mr. and Mrs. Devil Demon were in the shop.

They were beautiful mannequins or life-sized dolls. They were both scary—and captivating.

Danni walked around them and touched them. The way Quinn watched her as she did so made her wonder if he had already done the same thing.

She could feel nothing.

Certainly, nothing evil.

"There were dozens of *things* in the house and in the yard," Quinn told her. "These were just the most—real?"

"They are fantastic," Danni agreed. She hesitated. They usually kept *The Cheshire Cat* open late during Halloween season. That night, she'd decided the day had been far too long; she'd put the "closed" sign up at nine.

Billie was whipping up a very late dinner; Bo Ray was making sure the guest room was ready. She and Quinn were alone in the shop.

Danni shivered suddenly.

"What? The dolls?"

She shook her head. "No…just…just Halloween," she said. "But, I do suggest we, too, play jazz music tonight. And, of course, make sure we lock the door between the shop and the rest of the house."

Wolf barked.

He seemed to be in absolute agreement.

Chapter 6

"What's for dinner?" Quinn asked Billie, stepping into the kitchen.

Sean and Casey had arrived; they'd been shown to their temporary room upstairs.

Billie cast him an aggravated glare, shaking his head, his long, thin white hair swaying as he did so. "Dinner! At almost ten at night. Haggis, that's what it should be, boy!"

"Haggis?"

Quinn was startled by Billie's words. Haggis was a traditional Scot's dish, yes, but made using a sheep's or a calf's heart, liver, and lungs and other parts, and—as long as Quinn had known Angus and Billie!—it had never been served in the house on Royal Street.

"Haggis," Quinn repeated.

Billie let out a sound of aggravation. "Shepherd's pie, my friend, using only some ground beef and pork, good potatoes, and some seasoning. Peas and corn on the side—Angus never liked peas mixed in with his meat. By the way, haggis—and shepherd's pie, for that matter—are rather like pizza."

"Like pizza?"

"They were cheap and easy to make, made from the leftovers, after good cuts of meat had been sold. And, Angus never did like haggis, be he a Scot or nae. He said he worked hard for a living and could afford better food. So, bring your guests on down. Time for dinner. Now, if ye've a problem with shepherd's pie..."

Quinn lifted a hand. "Not a problem in the world! Sounds delicious. At this point, even the haggis sounded good. None of us have eaten in a very long time!"

"I'll call the others," Quinn said.

He crashed into Bo Ray in the hall.

"They're all set," Bo Ray said. "Room is spiffy clean with new sheets, yada, yada. And you and Danni saw the shop was all locked. Dinner—and then I'm to bed. Long day!"

"Yep, long day," Quinn agreed. "Go on in, I'll run up for Danni and our guests.

He found Danni, Wolf, and Casey and Sean in the broad hall that separated the upstairs room and held the second set of stairs that led to the attic apartments. Danni had been helping them get to know Wolf, which was easy enough.

Wolf was lapping up the attention.

"He's as big as a small horse!" Casey said, smiling as Quinn reached the hallway.

"Best dog ever," Quinn said, patting Wolf's head. "And we have some dinner downstairs; I know I'm ready for it."

"Let's go," Danni said.

She led the way. Casey followed her. Sean tapped Quinn's shoulder. "Thank you!" he told him. "I can't thank you enough."

"It's okay. We want to get to the truth here, too, Sean. This is an easy enough fix for you and Casey now." He shrugged. "I actually own a house, too. But, I have renters in it now, so...anyway, I hope Casey will feel better here."

"She's already herself again!" Sean said happily. "I just don't know...and, I'm worried about us. And a man was killed. A man who never hurt anyone."

"It's a tragedy," Quinn said. "And, I'm afraid, others may die. Unless we catch this killer. So, we have to do everything we can—follow anything that looks like a lead." He studied Sean. "I'm going to have to talk to your friends—Chrissy and Gill. They may know something—they may have seen something—and not even realize it."

"Hey, you guys!" Danni called. "Dinner!"

"Let's get down there, huh?" Quinn said.

They headed down to dinner. Billie was on the grouchy side, telling them they were eating on paper plates, and that's the way it was. But, Casey really was a sweet young woman. She immediately laughed and told him she ate on paper plates all the time, and his shepherd's pie was so good, she'd be happy to eat it out of a cooking bowl. Billie became friendlier.

Bo Ray was thrilled to meet Casey. "I've seen your name on some of the cards you've created!" he told her.

When dinner was over, Quinn told Casey and Sean to get some sleep. Danni insisted she could clean up, so Billie and Bo Ray could get some sleep. Quinn helped her, and they were done and upstairs within ten minutes.

He closed the door to their room and heard Wolf settle down in the hallway—the place he always kept guard.

When the door was closed, Danni immediately turned into his arms.

"I think we're alone now!" she whispered.

He laughed softly, stroking her hair.

"I do love being alone," he whispered.

She ran a finger down the length of his chest and leaned in and kissed him.

He kissed her deeply in return. In a few minutes, they were entwined, laughing as they stripped one another of their clothing, falling together on the bed.

They'd learned long ago that in the world they lived in, they needed one another.

And needed one another in this way.

"I just love the taste of..." he whispered, kissing her.

"Hm, my flesh?" she whispered.

"I was thinking of crème brulee," he said.

"Um, and when I touch you..."

"You're amazed by my muscle and prowess?"

"I'm amazed to realize I'm thinking of dusty brick."

"Dusty brick?" He laughed softly.

"Maybe I love dusty brick!

She rolled in his arms. Their whispers teased as they kissed and touched intimately and erotically. And in her arms, he could forget the ugliness in the world, and see only beauty.

"I love you," she whispered, and he returned the words passionately.

Then the teasing was over, and the sounds they made weren't really words at all, until sensation erupted in an incredible high, physical climax, both hearts and bodies afire, and slowly, slowly cooling. Quinn held her close, beyond grateful he had found her and they were together in the world.

She was curled snugly in his arms, and he just held her. For a bit, there was just the sweetness of lying there

And then, of course, the day came back. He felt it when Danni fell asleep; he began to doze himself. And then he awoke with a start.

Danni was up. Sleek and beautiful, she was headed for the door.

And he knew where she was going, and what she was doing.

He jumped up himself, slid into pajama bottoms, and raced after her with a robe. She was halfway down the stairs.

He was careful as he slipped the robe around her shoulders. She slept walked—and she slept painted. And she was headed down to her studio to do so, he knew.

He cursed himself for being an idiot; the house was asleep, but still...he should have thought to have made sure they threw on robes or pajamas after...

That didn't matter. Couldn't matter. There was a killer on the prowl.

Wolf followed; when Danni went into her studio, Quinn followed and told the dog, "Watch this door, boy!"

Wolf sat before the door. Quinn closed it.

Danni was heading straight for her easel where she'd set a fresh canvas. She began to sketch. She was a good artist; she created many fantastic pieces, but perhaps none as fantastic as those that came through when she was sleep-sketching or painting.

He waited and watched. Her strokes began to create a picture, but, he frowned, trying to decipher the drawing first, and then the meaning. She'd drawn a fireplace, with an armchair before it. An old man sat in the chair, a book open before him, and a young child by his side, looking at the book.

It seemed like something out of a Norman Rockwell painting at first.

And then he saw the portrait in an oval frame above the fireplace. The portrait was of a man in a slouch hat, dark suit, and lowered head. His flesh had begun to decay. He had an evil grin on his face, as if he enjoyed what he was seeing. The painting above the hearth seemed all the more malignant because of the charming scene of the man and the child.

The sketch was apparently finished. Danni dropped her pencil, staring at, but not seeing, her canvas.

She rose, letting the robe he'd gotten her slip from her shoulders. He quickly retrieved and walked up to her before she could open the door to the hall. She stood acquiescent as he slipped it on to her.

He held her then by the shoulders. "Danni, Danni!" he said softly.

For a moment, she still just stared. Then she blinked, and she saw him. She gasped softly.

"Oh, no, did I..."

"It's fine. You came down here okay, just me behind you. You're in your robe."

"What did I draw? Or was I painting?"

"A sketch."

She pulled away from him, hurrying to stand before the easel.

"What the hell?" She murmured

He pointed to the painting above the fireplace in her sketch.

"That looks like one of the descriptions given of the Axeman. A decayed Axeman, but, nevertheless..."

"He'd be dead; he'd have to be dead," she said softly. "A portrait over the mantle...." She turned to look at Quinn. "Someone out there...knows something about the Axeman that we don't."

"His identity?" Quinn asked dryly.

"You're being a wise-ass, but, yes. Quinn, don't you think someone believes they're his descendent, at the very least."

"Yes, that's not a stretch. But, the thing is...the creatures. The insects and animals that rip up the bodies now. That didn't happen with the original Axeman. Although..."

"What?"

"The Axeman is dead. So...insects and vultures come around as a body decays."

"And squirrels?" she asked.

"Maybe they're just part of the bargain."

"Natasha said there was a woman in—"

"Her Medusa."

"Yes, and she was asking about spells to wake the dead."

"Great," he murmured.

"Well, it is getting us somewhere. We have to find her."

"Yep. Find Medusa."

Danni grimaced.

"For now...it's about three A.M. Let's try to get some sleep."

She nodded, thoughtful.

They were going back to bed—to sleep.

In pajamas, Quinn determined.

They started out of the studio. Wolf suddenly started to bark. Quinn hurried out into the hallway.

Wolf, hackles raised, was staring at the door to the shop.

"What is it, boy?" Quinn demanded. Striding forward, he threw open the door.

The shop was quiet. Nothing was amiss. But...

He could hear footsteps out on the sidewalk. Someone hurrying away.

"Quinn?" Danny asked.

"Nothing." He flicked on the shop lights. No one was in the shop; nothing had changed.

He didn't think.

Danni brushed by him, walking into the center of the shop. And there, she seemed to freeze.

"Quinn?"

"What is it?"

"They—they moved!"

She was referring to Mr. and Mrs. Devil Demon. And he wasn't sure, but she might have been right. The thing was they seemed to have moved toward the door of the shop, as if...

"It's as if they're on guard there, protecting the shop," Danni said, her voice soft and perplexed.

Two voices. Casey Cormier had heard two voices, one urging her out, one urging her to stay.

He walked up to the mannequins and studied them both. Their faces hadn't changed. And, yet, he was certain Danni was right. It was subtle, but there was something different.

"Is it possible for a spirit of goodness to inhabit something, too?" Danni whispered.

"Maybe," Quinn said. "Why not? I mean, if there is evil, there is also...goodness. But, if so...if these guys are good, just what the hell was at Sean's that was evil?"

***

Natasha called Danni's cell, bright and early. She'd phoned Father Ryan already, and Father Ryan would be at her place by 7:30 A.M.

They needed to meet, to find out if anyone had any information the others didn't. "I figured my courtyard was best, and really early was best. You have houseguests, and we may not want them hearing everything, so, my place. And this way, we can have Jez and Bo Ray, and then they can get back to keeping shop if...if we need to be elsewhere," Natasha said.

"Sounds good," Danni told her. Quinn was already up, looking at her. She thought he could hear Natasha, and if not, he knew what was going on.

He was out of bed before Danni could hang up.

"What about our guests?" she asked.

"We leave them sleeping."

"What if they wake up?"

"We leave a note."

He was already in the shower. She thought about joining him, and then decided to wait. When he was out, she hurried in.

By 7:20, they had wakened Billie and Bo Ray, and they were all ready to take the short walk down to Natasha's.

Father Ryan had beaten them there. And he wasn't alone.

Father Ryan—a bull of a man who was a damned good Catholic priest, even if he was on the unorthodox side—had called on another of their strange associates. He was there with Hattie Lamont, the very rich widow with whom they'd become involved while working on the case of the bloody Hubert painting. Hattie was both elegant, authoritative—and somehow down to earth as well. She was in her sixties or early seventies, Danni had figured, but she could move with the grace of a teenager and carry herself with complete dignity.

Hattie had also learned the hard way that the world could be very strange.

"Hattie!" Danni said, hugging her, and then Father Ryan.

"You weren't going to invite me?" Hattie queried, smiling.

"Actually, I was going to call you," Quinn said.

Hattie sighed. "He has a favor to ask," she told Danni.

"I do. How do you feel about turning your place on Esplanade into a Halloween wonderland—for kids from the schools."

"You know I'm all in on that," Hattie said.

"Of course, she is!" Father Ryan said. "Got to get moving here—I have a mass this morning!"

"Yes, yes, of course!" Hattie said. "Quinn, we'll talk after."

Quinn nodded his thanks to Hattie. They gathered around the table, Danni, Quinn, Billie, and Bo Ray, Father Ryan, Hattie, Natasha, and Jez.

"Sean DeMille is one of my parishioners," Father Ryan. "He called me yesterday right after he called the police, and, naturally...I told him to call you, Quinn. So...?" He lifted his hands, looking around the table.

"So!" Quinn said. He related the events that had occurred with him. Danni went on to tell them what she had discovered in her father's book, and about visiting Eric Garfield. Quinn told them about *Horrible Hauntings,* and how he believed someone had lured Sean DeMille from his home. He also mentioned Mr. and Mrs. Devil Demon, and how they didn't seem to be malignant, but...

They had moved. And someone had been in the street.

Now, it was New Orleans, so, someone being on Royal Street at 3:00 A.M. didn't necessarily mean anything.

Natasha had Jez told them about his "Medusa" woman.

And Danni went on to relay information about the "sleep-sketching" she had done, something they all knew about.

"It appears what we have is someone channeling the Axeman," Father Ryan said. "In what way—we need to know—and the 'who' on that would be very helpful, very helpful, indeed."

Danni spoke carefully. "In other words...it's not just an object that came from someone evil, but we might we looking at something similar to what we've seen before. Someone is—or thinks they are—a descendent of the Axeman, and somehow, they've delved into his...power?"

"Could it be the same person, though?" Natasha asked. "Danni, Eric Garfield told you about murders in 1942 and in 1972. And the Axeman was 1918 through 1919."

"A dynasty!" Quinn said softly. He leaned forward. "Which could just make it easier for us!"

"How?" Jez asked.

"We have more than the present—we have the past. If we can find out more about the people involved in the past, we can perhaps find out who followed after them into our present day."

"I can work with Eric Garfield again," Danni said.

Quinn agreed with Danni to continue searching through the archives.

"The only woman I know of who was involved in this from the start is Chrissy Monroe, a friend of Casey's, who works with her. I think I should see her—and her boyfriend, Gill

Martin. They were at the house when I went over with Larue. I already saw Ned Denton—and *Horrible Hauntings.*"

"I'll go through parish files," Father Ryan said, "and call in favors from friends." He paused. "I've started, but now I'll have a better idea of where I'm going."

"And we'll get word out," Natasha said.

"That's it, then, let's move," Quinn said. He started to rise.

"Quinn!" Father Ryan said, stopping him. "I'll talk to Hattie about Sean DeMille's work with the schools—for Halloween for the children." He hesitated. "I know Sean DeMille. I've known him since he was a kid. I'd bet my life he's not involved in any way—other than he might have been targeted. Or Casey might have been targeted."

Quinn smiled. "Thank you."

"I'm going to love this," Hattie said. "I'll be useful in all, too."

"Hattie, you're always a gem!" Danni told her.

"We'd best be moving, indeed," Billie said. "Bo Ray and I need to be getting the shop open; murder doesn't stop shoppers or tourists—not just one murder, anyway."

They all rose, ready to go their separate ways. As they walked back to the shop, Quinn told Danni, "Wolf goes with you—wherever you go."

"Of course!" she promised him.

When they reached the house on Royal Street, he gave her a quick kiss on the head.

Nothing like his kisses of the night before!

He paused for a minute in the shop, looking at Mr. and Mrs. Devil Demon.

He looked at Danni. "Maybe they shouldn't be here," he said.

"And maybe they should be," Danni said.

"They don't bother me any," Bo Ray said cheerfully. "I like them!"

"Billie?" Quinn asked.

"Wolf seems okay; I'm okay," Billie said.

"All right, then...." Quinn studied the characters again, then headed out through the house.

."I'm going back to see Eric Garfield; Wolf and I will just walk," she told Billie and Bo Ray.

"What about Casey and Sean?"

"They can help themselves to whatever they need, go to work...come and go," Danni said. "You can reach me easily and I can be back here quickly. I'm just a short walk up past Rampart."

"All right, and be calling if you need us!" Billie said firmly.

"Oh, that lady was coming back by to see if we'd carry her jack-o-lanterns," Bo Ray said.

"She's a little late, but...just have her leave one. And I'll call her and let her know if I think we can move them for her. We're very close to Halloween."

"Last minute rush!" Bo Ray said.

Danni curled Wolf's leash around her hand. He was a good boy; he'd stay with her no matter what, but he always went out on a leash anyway.

"Okay, then we're off!" she said. Waving to Billie and Bo Ray, she left the shop and headed out on Royal.

She looked back.

It was almost as if they were watching her. Mr. and Mrs. Devil Demon.

With either care or concern...

Or with the deepest malice and most evil intent?

Chapter 7

Quinn called Larue from the car.

"You get anything on James Hornby? Any friends who have any idea of how he got to the Garden District?" Quinn asked him.

"I talked to the business owners on the street. It was sad. Everyone loved the guy. He could go into any of the restaurants and get a hand out. He was even offered places to stay. He always said thank you, and maybe he'd spend a night somewhere, but he didn't accept anything more than that."

"Where was he sleeping then?" Quinn asked.

"Different places. A guy who owns a donut shop said he knew a lot of people who told him he could bunk down in the garages, porches, or even their homes. He would do so now and then, and take showers at shelters, and things like that. It seems he didn't want to become beholden to one place or person. He would, however, so they said, takes rides here and there. I found a dozen or so people who knew him and cared about him; I couldn't find one person who knew of a specific friend in the Garden District who he might have been visiting or seeing. Spent the whole day on the street. And what I learned is he probably took a ride with someone to go somewhere."

"No one remembers seeing him get in a car with anyone?"

"Busy street; busy season. No. Donut guy said he gave him one of his new specials to try out—but that was early. People with an antique shop saw him opening their door for a lady with a cane at about 4:00. Others remember seeing him on the street, but that's all. How did you do?"

Quinn told him what he suspected about the coffin being purposely rigged to lure Sean out of the house.

"They lured Sean away—to kill a man in his yard? They didn't want to kill Sean—or Casey?"

"Maybe it was just a taunt." Quinn was quiet a second. He was always careful about what he said to Larue and others. He never wanted to put his old partner in an uncomfortable position, or one in which others could tease him about working with the haunts of New Orleans or the vampire brigade, or so on.

"I don't know. Jake, how long did you interview those friends of Sean's—Gill Martin and Chrissy Monroe? I'm headed out to *Paper People*. I'm going to speak with Chrissy now."

"At her work?"

"Hey, I'll be good. Thing is, I talked to Natasha, asked her if there was any mumbling in her circles about someone abusing voodoo, looking for spells that cause evil, that kind of a thing." He told Larue about the "Medusa" woman.

"I talked to them both for a while. They showed up at the scene *after* I got there, and after Hubert was on the scene, too. They talked about that night; they were all there. They weren't drinking at all—coffee, milk, and cookies. They left, Sean left...I had no grounds to stand on to drag them down to the station—or suspect they might have come over to kill someone." He sighed. "But, hey, you do your no-I'm-not-a-cop thing and see what you can get from her."

"I'll be careful," Quinn promised.

"Weird, Quinn. The way that body was chewed up."

"Well, creatures...chew dead bodies. Thing is, I'm hoping to hell someone isn't trying to bring back the Axeman."

Larue made some kind of a strange sound.

"Danni is going to be over with Eric Garfield today—we think it might be a descendent of the Axeman."

"Well, I'll just look that right up!" Larue said with weary sarcasm. "No one knows who the Axeman was!"

"Yeah, I know."

Larue was quiet. He groaned. "I'm going to see what I can find in the records, though, I'm assuming, Eric Garfield will have it all together. He and his dad...that case was an obsession with them. You never know what might hit though; talk to me after you visit with Chrissy Monroe. And, I'm assuming, you're going to try to talk to Gill Martin. I've talked to them; my men have talked to them...we've got nothing. Just a dead man with an axe in his head, chewed up by creatures that don't usually chew on corpses—the squirrels, anyway. The guy was a vet. Maybe he was dying of cancer, but the least we can give him is justice."

"And we'll do it. We know someone picked him up off the street, so, I'm thinking, local, someone he knew. That person got him to Sean's and Casey's house where he hit him with the axe and got the hell out but not before somehow taunting Casey out to see the body. I'm saying someone who knew Sean and Casey because they had to have gotten into the house to do the voices and the taunting."

"So you're back to..."

"Someone at *Horrible Hauntings,* or someone who was a close friend."

"I'll do some more work on your Axeman, and try Magazine Street again," Larue said. "If you're right, and someone is trying to pull an Axeman in the city..."

"I know."

"Keep me up to date."

"Will do."

Quinn ended the call. He'd reached the offices of *Paper People.*

***

"Let's go back to the first incident after the original Axeman attacks," Danni said to Garfield. "That was when the soldier was found dead in the bayou by his wife—who was arrested and then let go. But, her husband was never seen again."

"Gretchen and Nathan Amory," Eric Garfield said.

"She was left with a household of children, right?"

"Yes."

"Did the family stay in the area?" Danni asked.

Garfield picked up one of his folders and handed it to Danni. "Looks like the kids had enough of the swamp. I followed up on them. Gretchen stayed in the area, but the kids moved on out—New York City and L.A. I guess they wanted the city lights."

"Okay," Danni said. "So, we move on to the case in 1972."

Eric nodded his head. "Sure. Okay. Barry Alexander was the victim. Tourist found by another tourist. But, his body also disappeared."

"And he wasn't local."

"Nope. He was from Mississippi."

"Okay, but there were other murders at the time of each."

"Right. Gordon Hampton was found in an abandoned bar."

"And later—in 1972—the murder that occurred then was chalked up to a cult."

"I've researched that as far as I could. Seven members were arrested and went to prison. Not one of them is alive today. Two died of cancer; three committed suicide in prison. One died of heart failure, and another inmate knifed one of them to death. The thing is—even then, records seemed to disappear. And I don't think the police were involved. I really don't."

"We need names," Danni said. "Names to cross-reference."

"What do you mean?"

"Okay, the majority of people thought the Axeman was someone named Mumfre or Munfre or something of a twist on that name. If we take all of the names—all those we have—and cross reference them with the different decades, we just might have something."

Eric shook his head. He quoted softly from the Axeman's presumed letter. "'*They have never caught me and they never will. They have never seen me, for I am invisible, even as the ether that surrounds your earth. I am not a human being, but a spirit and a demon from the hottest hell. I am what you Orleanians and your foolish police call the Axeman*'"

Danni looked at him and said softly, "There was someone flesh and blood murdering people. We don't really know what 'evil' is—not when it comes to flesh and blood. Sure, it exists— we all know that. We see it in a million acts of bloodshed and cruelty. But, there's someone out there unleashing whatever this is. Eric, help me, we need to find out what is going on."

He nodded and leaned forward, reaching for his laptop.

"I'm on it. I'm going to give you a list of names. But...how the hell are you going to connect them? People move about. They change their names. I just don't see how we can do this, but..."

"We're working an angle, all right?"

He smiled at her. "If we could get some answers...and, if there is a Heaven, my dad is there. But, wherever he is, I know he'd be damned glad if we could get to the bottom of this!"

"Whatever we find," Danni said softly. "It won't really prove the identity of the Axeman in 1918-1919. I mean, even if a crazed person—descendent or not—is using what they believe to kill now, we'd have nothing that would stand up in court for the past."

Eric Garfield smiled. "But, we'll know!" he said. "I'll know—and I like to believe my dad will know."

***

The receptionist at *Paper People* smiled prettily when Quinn entered the offices." How can we help you, sir? It's not too late for Thanksgiving or Christmas banners!"

"I hear you do the best work in the city," Quinn said. The girl beamed.

"We have the most innovative designers on the planet!" She said enthusiastically.

"Actually, at the moment, I just wanted to speak with Casey Cormier and Chrissy Monroe. Are they in yet?"

"Casey just got here, and Chrissy came in early. They are two of our best, but..."

"Thank you. Through that doorway?"

"I should announce you—"

"That's okay."

Quinn hurried through the doorway that led to the design studio.

Chrissy and Casey were both at their desks—desks that faced one another in a large room.

Casey looked at him with surprise and concern. "Is everything all right?" She asked him anxiously. "We found your note on the table and just locked the kitchen door when we left."

"Everything is fine. I'm sorry we were all gone when you woke up." He saw Chrissy had stopped whatever work she was doing and was watching the exchange. "I just wanted to make sure you got in okay."

He turned to Chrissy. "And, I was hoping to speak with you, too!"

"Me?" Chrissy said, sounding confused.

"I was hoping you might have remembered something. A car on the street, maybe."

"A car on the street?"

"Yes, Detective Larue believes that James Hornby was given a ride to Casey's house."

"Why would he want a ride to my house?" Casey asked.

"Well, he liked to find different places to sleep at night," Quinn said. "He didn't want to owe people, so he moved around. Poor man. He was an easy mark."

"I wish I could help!" Chrissy said. She shook her head. "I don't know. Gill and I were there, and we were all having a great time. Then we went home. When we left..."

"Were there cars in the road?"

"Yes, I remember a fair amount of traffic on St. Charles Street," Chrissy said. "But...I don't remember anything specific. I'm so sorry."

"You and Gill went home, right home?"

"We did. It was a work night."

He walked around to her side of the double desks and smiled as he looked down at her computer. She was working on a Christmas banner.

"Cool," he said.

"I'm glad to be working on Christmas!" Chrissy told him.

"Neat place here," he said, indicating the studio. "Who decided who does what here?"

"Oh, our boss in Cleveland sends down the assignments," Chrissy told him. "He hires and fires and all that."

"We have a manager here, of course, but, she's really just an office manager. She keeps us all on our toes," Casey said.

Chrissy hit a key on her computer, and her computer screen popped up with a giant spider web that held jack-o-lanterns and grinning skeletons and more.

"Wow, that's wonderful. You did that?" Quinn asked.

Chrissy smiled. "My Halloween screen saver," she said. She looked around and then at Casey. "We should be getting back to work!"

"Not to worry; I might have been looking for some advertising for *The Cheshire Cat!*" Quinn said. "Hey, is Gill a designer, too?"

"A designer?" Chrissy asked.

"You three are so artistic...I thought he might be, too."

Casey smiled. "He's the most artistic of all of us. He's an electrician. He is great, though. Amazing, and I'm serious. Very talented. He's helped out with a lot of the local theater groups."

"Nice."

"Chrissy, if I need anything more..."

"Come and talk to me any time. Well, don't get me in trouble at work!" she added. "And if I can think of anything, of course, I'll let you know immediately. That poor man!"

Quinn thanked them both again.

"And thank you, thank you and Danni so much for letting us stay at your place!" Casey told him. She stood to walk out with him.

He turned to wave to Chrissy. She was still watching him. He smiled.

Casey had his arm as they headed to the door. "I just wanted to thank you, all, too, for Mrs. Lamont. Hattie Lamont. She called Sean this morning; he's doing a set-up in her yard, and he's making it really simple. Kids will get to come by. It will be a day late, but...he's so happy. I mean, not happy! We're all heart-broken that a man is dead, but the kids do love what Sean does, and..."

"Hattie is great. I'm so glad it worked out. Do you know where Gill is working?"

"Oh, yes, it's over on the Haggerty project—revamping another old warehouse into a storage facility. Air-conditioned—and upper crust," Casey said. "He's a great guy. He and Chrissy are so in love. I met Chrissy through work, of course, and then we met Gill, and we do lots of things together. Gill was going to help Sean finish up the yard, and, I'm sure, he'll help him at Mrs. Lamont's house over on Esplanade. This is really so nice of her."

"Hattie is great," Quinn agreed. He hesitated, wanting to move carefully.

"Do you and Chrissy ever have trouble at work?"

"Me and Chrissy? Oh, lord, no! We help each other all the time."

"Great to hear," Quinn said. "Well, I don't want to get you fired. I'll see you back at the house later, and..."

"And?"

"If anyone frightens you, or if you don't want to be alone, just call."

She smiled. "Sean is with Mrs. Lamont now, but, he's going to pick me up after work."

"Great," Quinn said.

He headed on out, making his way to the warehouse where Gill Martin was working.

He noted that it was close—very close—to the old warehouse that had been turned into *Horrible Hauntings*.

Before finding a parking spot, Quinn put a call through to Larue.

"Yeah? You got something?"

"Nothing but suspicion," Quinn told him. "Can you do background checks on Gill Martin and Chrissy Monroe, *and* on Ned Denton and Jeff Abernathy?"

"All right. I did a bit or research already. Chrissy came here from Santa Fe when she was about ten, and Gill arrived from NYC six years ago. Neither has anything but parking tickets."

"Santa Fe and NYC, thanks. What about their parents?"

"I didn't go that far back. What makes you so suspicious about that pair? We're probably looking for a maniac."

"The charming maniac from next door," Quinn murmured. "Had to be someone close. Someone who had been in the house."

"Unless Casey Cormier was a little freaked out—and therefore a little unhinged," Larue said.

"Sure. There's that. But, I think I'm right."

"I'll get back on it," Larue promised.

"Them and Abernathy and Denton."

"You got it."

They ended the call. Quinn found parking a block and half away and walked back to the old warehouse that was being revamped.

He surveyed the construction site. It was hard-hat with warning signs around it. Not a great place to try to speak with Gill Martin.

Still, he found the contractor working at a table in front. He asked him if there was a break time, or a few seconds in there when he could speak with Gill.

"Sure—except that Gill isn't here. He didn't show up this morning; I've called, but, I'm not getting anything."

Quinn thanked him and started back to the car. He had barely done so when his phone rang.

It was Larue.

"You got something this fast?" Quinn asked.

"Yeah. A dead man, in a coffin—at *Horrible Hauntings.*"

"Who?"

"Well, I won't have to check up on Jeff Abernathy. He's the man in the coffin.

Chapter 8

"I've found something!" Danni cried, turning to Eric Garfield.

He looked up from his own studies.

Wolf barked excitedly.

"Your dad referred to Gretchen Avery with her maiden name in one of his notes," she said excitedly. "Her maiden name was Gaffney."

"Okay," Eric said, looking at her blankly.

"Gaffney was married to a woman named *Mathilda Manfre.*"

"All right. That could be another version of Munfre or Mumfre," Eric agreed. "But, what? She did murder her husband. And she tried to get away with it by having the gators chew up the body. And she had a streak in her that was sick..."

"And that's why her children left the area."

"That was 1942."

"And the murders started up again in 1972."

"Was she still alive?"

"I don't know. I mean, she could have been. And her children would have been in their twenties or even their thirties by then. We need to find those kids," Danni told him.

As she spoke, her phone rang. It was Quinn, and he was tense.

"Second murder," he told her grimly.

"Where?"

"At *Horrible Hauntings.* The owner himself; he was found in the same coffin that Sean was called in to fix the night before last."

"And there was...an axe in his head?" she asked.

Eric was studying her, shaking his head sadly.

"Yes. And..."

"And?"

"The coffin was filled with roaches and rats. I'm here now, Danni. Hubert is going to give us an approximate time of death. He never gives a real statement until autopsy, but he believes the axe blow killed the man immediately and the...chewing came after death."

"Quinn, we may be on to something. I might have found a thread to follow from way back."

"You know who it might be?"

"Not yet, I need a little time."

"He's going to strike again, Danni. The Axeman's copycat is going to strike again."

"I know, I know. We're working it...as fast as we can."

"Wolf is with you?"

"Yes, of course."

"Danni, can I be heard?"

She hesitated. Eric Garfield was a good distance from her.

"I don't believe so."

"Please, as soon as you can, get back to the shop. I want you with Billie and Bo Ray and Wolf, all in one place, safe—and damned close to Natasha and Jez. Please."

"I need a little more time here, Quinn. And..."

She let her voice trail. Had Quinn suddenly become suspicious of Eric Garfield?

She couldn't say that aloud.

"Just a little time. I'll call when I'm leaving."

"Thanks. Thanks, and please. Please leave quickly."

"I will, I will...but, I'm almost there, Quinn. I'm almost there!"

"I need you almost home," Quinn said softly.

"Of course, of course, I'll meet you there!"

She hung up and looked over at Eric Garfield. He was just sitting in his chair, studying his notes.

He looked up. "Quinn's okay, right?"

"There's been another murder. At *Horrible Hauntings.*"

"I knew it," Garfield said dismally. "I knew he would keep working!"

Danni was suddenly nervous. Quinn! Damn him. Garfield had been a cop—a detective—like his father. They'd studied the cases. They'd tried to solve them.

He was helping her now!

"He needs me back at the house soon for something," she said.

Did she really need the man's notes anymore? What she had to do now had to do with working the Internet and public records.

"I guess I'd better head back now," she said. "Eric, thank you. I can't tell you how helpful you've been."

"I'm here anytime you need," he said. "And, I swear, I'll keep at it!"

He was so damned sincere.

She left Eric's house with Wolf.

She didn't call Quinn back until she'd cleared Rampart Street.

"Danni?" he asked anxiously, hearing her voice. "Where are you?"

"Out of there, and on my way to the shop. What the hell, Quinn? Are you suspicious of Eric Garfield?"

"I don't know. I just know the paper called the police station; they received a letter. From the 'New Age Axeman.'"

"Oh—are they sure it's...the killer?"

"Oh, yeah. It hasn't been published yet, and the killer threatens a bloodbath by Halloween. Like the last letter, he asks that everyone play jazz. Says Satan loves jazz."

"What does that have to do with Eric?"

"I'll read you the letter," he said. "'New Orleans, I'm back! Strong and sleek, no hiding in the bayou. One down in the garden, and one in a coffin where he belonged. Am I a *sir* this life. Or a *ma'am?* Or perhaps I am an earl. King of the dead, as it may be, the hunter and the hunted, and the spirit who will escape all. You'll see me and be blind. For I am that spirit, he who cleanses the streets, and my night is coming, for I am the strongest of the spirits, and I will prevail on that night when the dead awaken."

"The language is nothing like that in the original letter!" Danni said.

"Well, the killer may be channeling a spirit somehow, but he's still flesh and blood."

"Or she," Danni said.

"Or she," Quinn agreed. "We have to solve his. The night of the dead...Halloween. We're just days ahead."

"Just days," Danni agreed.

"Anyway, please, get to the shop!"

"On my way," she said, and added, "Quinn, the killer may know that Eric Garfield—like his father—has been investigating the case. He could be in danger."

"He could be."

"Then—"

"Not to worry, Danni. Larue is sending patrol cars to keep watch over him today."

***

Jeff Abernathy lay in the horror house coffin, his eyes open, an expression of surprise on his face—and an axe sticking out of his skull.

Police and forensics had done their best to capture the insects and rodents crawling over his body; he, like James Hornby, had been gnawed on voraciously.

Hubert, stood, shaking his head. "I've never seen anything like it. A body left in the bayou, yes. A body in the elements for years and years, yes. But...Mr. Hornby, and now this? I can't figure it."

Quinn turned to Larue. The place was very quiet; lights were on everywhere.

"Who called it in?" he asked. There was only one skinny looking kid, white-faced and leaned against the wall in the room, who appeared to be an employee.

Larue looked at him. "Abernathy!" he said.

"Abernathy?" Quinn queried.

"Yep, he called the cops saying he'd come in to check the place out—and he was afraid someone was in here who shouldn't be. We sent Officer Tarleton over there to check it out. The door was open—we're lucky we didn't wind up with a dozen crazy teens in here—and Tarleton walked in and followed the path and found the body."

Tarleton was one of the police officers in the room, keeping their distance from the coffin itself and trying to stay out of the way of the forensic team that was busy working.

"Tarleton?" Larue said, calling the man.

Tarleton walked over to Quinn and Larue.

"Please go over what you did when you arrived," Quinn asked.

"Yes, sir. Mr. Quinn, I came in by the open door. I admit, I knew the maze of pathways—been here with my wife. I didn't touch anything—except the door to come in. I just kept calling for Mr. Abernathy. And then I found him. Here." He swallowed. "As you see him."

"Thank you, Officer," Quinn said, and turned back to Larue again. "Where's his night manager—Ned Denton?" he asked.

"We've put a call in. He's due here any minute. I don't know why they call him the night manager—he's the only manager. Abernathy was the only one who came in here before five at night. From what I understand, Denton was always due in at about six, and all the actors came in about that time, too. Box office was supposed to be here around six, as well."

"I was here at night," Quinn told Larue. "I came to look at that coffin, and found fluff in it from one of the cloaks the backstage employees use when they have to come out and fix something. When I asked Sean what he fixed when he came in, he said someone had caught a bunch of the fabric in the gears. I still think that was done on purpose. But, the actor in here uses an axe—he's an executioner. Denton told me the axe was rubber. I believe it. So, this time, the murderer brought the axe with him. I sincerely doubt they had any real axes lying around."

"What do you think about the letter?" Larue asked him. "It arrived at the paper—or the paper called us!—at almost the exact same time we found Mr. Abernathy."

"I think this Axeman wants to be more famous than the original," Quinn said. "And, I think we really have to stop this bastard before Halloween."

There was a commotion from the back hallway; Ned Denton—accompanied by two policemen—burst into the room. He saw Abernathy in the coffin and gasped, sagging back so violently he had to be supported by the policemen.

"Oh, my God!" he exclaimed.

"He was a friend, as well as your boss?" Larue asked.

"Good friend—he trusted me when I was down and out. Good man!" Denton said in a whisper. "Oh, God!" he repeated, and turned away.

"Where were you after closing last night?" Quinn asked him.

"After closing?" he asked, as if he'd been attacked—and he was surprised. "Hell, home and in bed! I don't get out of here until about 4:00 A.M. I go home and go to bed, and then I...I wake up. And today...." He paused, swallowing hard. "I went into the Quarter for lunch. I ate on Chartres Street, near Jackson Square. I wandered around."

"Is there anyone who can vouch for you?" Larue asked.

Denton looked at him blankly.

"Did anyone see you?" Quinn asked. "And, lunch was a long time ago now. Where were you since then?"

"Home, I got dressed...." He was quiet for a minute, and then he beamed. "The cameras! The cameras were going, come into the security room. We can see the killer!"

"Perfect. Let's go," Larue said.

Back in the office with the wall of screens, they stared at footage of nothing—the place was closed during the day.

They could see when Abernathy arrived; he went into the office where they stood, and then began a systematic check of the rooms. They followed his movements, screen by screen.

They saw him enter the executioner's room, and come to look at the coffin.

And that's when the figure appeared. Entered the screen room, and then followed the same path Abernathy had taken.

"There!" Denton said. "There!"

Larue grunted.

Quinn watched silently. Yes, there was the murderer. They watched as he came up silently behind Jeff Abernathy, and slammed an axe into his head.

Thing was, they couldn't see a damned thing about the figure. The clothing was black—a shoulder-skirted jacket, pants, shoes—and large slouch hat.

"Run it again!" Larue barked.

And Denton did.

Never once did the figure's face appear. The black slouch hat hid the figure's features and even his skin tone in every single frame.

"I need this footage—all of it—for the crime lab," Larue said.

"Yes, sir, yes, sir, of course!" Denton said.

"One more time, please, before you pull it all for the police," Quinn asked.

And Denton showed it all one more time.

The killer had taken the axe from beneath his coat. He had brought it himself.

"Thank you," Quinn said. Larue nodded to him and they stepped out into the dark hallway again before either spoke.

Quinn asked Larue. "We'll at least get a height for the killer, right? Maybe a few more specifics on body type, at least?"

Larue nodded. "They'll do all kinds of things to the footage, you know that. Of course, the killer could have been wearing lifts in his shoes, and the coat or cape or whatever...pretty concealing. Still, we'll get something out of this."

Quinn already felt that he'd gotten something out of it. Thing was, it was just out of his touch. Somewhere, back burner, a clue tugged at him.

"Hubert will be taking the body to the morgue; autopsy tomorrow," Larue said. "Until then…"

"I'll be working," Quinn said quietly.

"I'm going to get specifics from Ned Denton. Find out where he was in detail. And, bring him in to the station with me, let him talk more there, see if his story remains the same. We'll grill him, get employee records, find out how many keys to the place there are out there."

"All right."

"You think he did this? Was all that horror an act?"

"It was a good one."

"Yeah, so—"

"So, I'm off to see a special haunted house for kids."

"What?"

"Sean DeMille. He's setting up for school kids at Hattie's house. He'll have some help there, I think. Gill Martin. Who, incidentally, didn't show up at work. But, maybe he was a no show because he decided to help Sean. I'll find out."

"All right. If you want to join in the interrogation with Mr. Denton here…"

"Thanks. I'll just see if I can find Mr. Martin, first. And I'll see how Danni's research into all this is going." He looked back toward the room where Denton was still working, procuring the footage for Larue.

"Let me know if his alibi does all pan out," Quinn said. "Too bad there were no cameras on the street. You think the killer was walking the CBD dressed like that?"

"Like the Axeman of 1918 and 1919?"

"He is dressed per the eye-witness descriptions they did have back then."

"You'd think someone would notice. But, hey, this is New Orleans. Worse—it's Halloween. Who the hell notices anything odd, here, at this time of year?"

Quinn headed on out.

He noted the sky. The day had passed in a blur.

Night was coming. Neon, parties, drinking, craziness…

And in the corners and the alleys...

Darkness. Shadows and darkness, both capable of hiding so very many sins.

***

Danni slipped into the courtyard and through the back door.

Billie was there when she entered, standing a fierce guard. He relaxed, seeing her and Wolf.

"Thank the good Lord that dog is back!" he said.

Danni laughed. "Thanks, Billie."

"My dear Danielle, you do not bark when something is a bit askew!" Billie told her.

"True. Has anything happened?"

"Not a thing. Business as usual. Bo Ray is handling it quite well. I've been...here. With Wolf now in residence, I'll be giving him more assistance."

"Thanks, Billie. I'll pop in on the shop, and then I'll be down in dad's room, searching through the book again."

Billie nodded and patted Wolf. "I've a fine piece of good steak for you, my friend. And then, well, you keep that nose of yours working on mischief, eh?"

Danni walked on through the hallway toward the shop, pausing at the door to her studio. She looked in, and then decided to study her sleep-sketch again.

The scene was so sweet...

Until it came to the portrait of the decaying man over the hearth.

"Who is it who thinks they have inherited your cause, whatever that may have been?" she wondered aloud, looking at the portrait. The Axeman.

She thought about the new letter the police had received. She wondered how many people would stay in—forgetting the Halloween holiday season—in fear of the Axeman.

Some would do so. They would check all their locks. They might even buy weapons.

Or big dogs.

But, most of the city would remain crazy, a gallery of victims for this copycat Axeman.

She headed out of the room, anxious to check on the shop, and then get back down to her father's book.

Her phone rang as she walked in. It was Natasha.

"Danni, a friend of mine called. Mack, who owns the voodoo shop down on Decatur."

"And?"

"Our costumed woman—Medusa—was in his place, too."

"Did she get what she wanted from him?"

"He doesn't do any of that black magic bull either," Natasha said. "But, she was telling a friend she knew someone down near Frenchmen Street who did. Thing is, Mack—my friend—told me he wasn't so sure our woman was a woman. Might have been a man dressed up as Medusa. I asked Jez, and Jez said, sure, it was possible. And, Jez said he knows the shop—it's run by a guy named Fred Ferrer, and he dabbles in all kinds of spells and things. Most of them bull, of course, but..."

"So, our killer might have found a spell. Thanks, Natasha. I'm heading back to the book."

"Anything more from Garfield?"

"I found a name that might relate. I just have to try to follow it!"

"I'm here if you need me," Natasha said.

Danni thanked her and headed on into the shop. Bo Ray was busy behind the counter, an old mahogany bar her dad had refitted as a counter.

He was smiling at a customer.

There were ten or so customers in the shop, several entranced by Mr. and Mr. Devil Demon.

Bo Ray completed a sale. Danni walked around the counter and asked him, "Anything—unusual?"

He shook his head. "Business as always," he said. "Busy—lots of sales. It's Halloween. Two people came by with crafts they'd like you to carry. That lady came by with her little jack-o-lanterns. Very cute. There at the end of the counter there. And a very young girl came in with some paintings. They're behind the counter, here. Pretty good. She's got a bit of twist in them, real with a hint of the fantastic. I think you'll like them."

"I'm sure I will," Danni said. She noted the jack-o-lanterns. They were about the size of an apple. Cute. Then she took a quick peek at the framed paintings behind the counter.

Everyone painted Jackson Square and the Cathedral. This girl had also painted the equestrian statue of Andrew Jackson—except that Jackson was tipping his hat. She quickly glanced at the other paintings. The young artist had also done her little bit with a mule drawn carriage—with a grinning mule, St. Louis #1—with a welcoming skeleton, and a view of the Mississippi—in which the river itself seemed to smile.

"Nice!" She told Billie. "Of course, we'll put them out and do our best for her! We can draw up paperwork tomorrow. I'm—I'm heading down to dad's office."

"You know, it is your office now," Billie said gently.

"Yes. And it will always be dad's office," she told him.

Several women were at the entrance of the shop, looking at the "Devil Demon" mannequins. Danni walked over to them.

"They're creepy!" one of them said.

"They're charming!" another countered.

Danni studied them again herself.

They were both; creepy and charming.

"Heading down; you know where to find me," Danni said, waving and calling out to Billie.

In her father's office, she sat behind the desk and opened the book. By rote she turned on the light—the lamp that flooded the pages of the book and sometimes showed what might not be seen without the intense light.

She re-read the pages she had already read. They verified everything she had learned from Eric Garfield.

She flipped more and more pages, time passing, as she sought more. And then, finally, she discovered an entry about "Bones of the Dead and the Cult of the Seven."

"'In the late sixties and early seventies, cults raged about the country. Mass suicides, the Manson murders, and more began to trend throughout the country, and parents prayed their children would not grow up to be swayed by such groups. The Cult of Seven arose in New Orleans. Their leader, Marc Henson, claimed to have the power of the super-being, not God, but a demon, and his followers believed that the demon could grant them good lives. Henson also claimed that he was the chosen one, selected from 'she who held the spirit before, who received it from he who had held it first.' Police began do investigate the members, and it was suspected that Henson would be arrested—and that there was evidence against him and he would face the death penalty. The cult members were found dead at their location near Slidell, all having taken cyanide.'"

Danni sat back, drumming her fingers on the desk.

Wolf wasn't with her—Billie had him doing guard duty by the kitchen door. She spoke aloud anyway; she'd become accustomed to talking to the dog.

"Okay, so, say that Gretchen Gaffney was really a Manfre, Mumfre, or Munfre...and there was such a person in the city of New Orleans during the Axeman spree. She would have known where his body was interred, and..."

She broke off. They had dealt with cases before in which the ashes of the dead had been worked into an object...such as the bust they'd dealt with when she and Quinn had first met. They'd been right from the beginning. Something in Casey and Sean's house had started it all.

Mr. and Mrs. Devil Demon? They were able to give off the appearance of being benign because they...they really were so evil?

If Danni was right, Manfre or Munfre had been the killer. His daughter had taken up after him—killed her husband, reported the killing...and, of course, gotten away with it.

"But who came after her?" she murmured.

She hesitated, then picked up the phone. She called Quinn.

"Where are you?" she asked him.

"Almost at Hattie's. Not far. Do you need me?"

"No, no. I think I'm almost at the end of the connection. I believe that the Axeman was a man named something like Mumfre, which became Manfre by the time his daughter married. She was Gretchen Avery and I believe she did kill her husband—and others. That was in the 1940s. I think she passed it on to a guy named Marc Henson, who was head of a cult. He died—cyanide when he was afraid he was going to be arrested."

"Good work! But after the 1970s?"

"That's what I'm looking for now. I need to know if Marc Henson left any descendants, of if anyone survived his cult...or if there's any way to figure a connection between someone now and Marc Henson back in the 70s."

"I'll get hold of Larue right away," Quinn told her. He hesitated. "You're home; you're safe—right?"

"Absolutely. I'm going to keep looking. You'd think this book would make it easier, wouldn't it?"

He was quiet for a minute. "I guess the book doesn't really know what's going to happen when."

"Hm. Okay. So..."

"I'll be back after I see what's happening at Hattie's."

"All right. Did—did Larue think Abernathy might have been killed by his manager?"

"Ned Denton is acting innocent as all hell. But, hey, he's got access. Larue is checking out the places he said he went during the day. But, I still say there was time. I don't know. I just don't know. I do say we're looking at Chrissy Monroe, Gill Martin—or, yes, Ned Denton. I was going to question Abernathy, but..."

"He's been proven innocent," Danni said softly.

"Yeah."

"I'll keep looking," Danni promised then hung up.

She turned back to the book. "Okay, if you were a computer, I'd key in 'evil ashes!'"

She flipped a few pages. And there it was. The exact heading.

Evil Ashes.

She kept reading.

Chapter 9

Darkness had fallen in earnest by the time Quinn reached Hattie Lamont's beautiful old home on Esplanade.

It had taken on quite a different appearance during the day. Sean's artistry was amazing. The friendly dinosaur stared down from the elegant and historical porch. Spider webs danced with grinning creatures within them. In a day, Sean DeMille had reset his entire display—adding more touches of pure fun, such as cherubic-looking witches and skeletons dancing to a popular jazz beat.

Hattie was out in the front with Sean.

And Gill Martin.

Hattie had an arm around Sean; she was speaking to him softly. As Quinn walked up to the trio, he knew, of course, what had so upset Sean.

He'd heard about Abernathy.

"Quinn, my God, have you heard?" Sean asked. "Jeff! Jeff Abernathy. He was a good man; a really good man. We had this just about up when I heard. It was great...Hattie is great...the kids...we could do all this for the kids. And now...it's my fault. It has to be my fault. I've done something, I don't know, but it was my house or Casey's house and then my work..."

"I'm sorry about Abernathy," Quinn said. "But, Sean, it's not your fault."

"We keep telling him that," Gill said. He looked at Quinn, shaking his head.

"Indeed," Hattie agreed. "Sean, I'm so sorry, too, but, tomorrow, children—children with wonderful lives ahead of them—will come here. And they'll see they can grow up and create things, tell stories...this is something wonderful. Despite the sickness of a killer, life goes on for others, and you're giving little ones a chance at some fun, needed in many little lives."

Gill looked at Sean. "Can't blame him—he worked for Abernathy."

That afternoon, Gill Martin looked like a later-day hippie. His hair was long and waving to his shoulders; he was wearing jeans and a T-shirt that advertised a 70s heavy metal band.

"So, Gill, you've been working this display all day with Sean?"

"Naw, I just got here in the afternoon."

"I couldn't have done the hard stuff without Gill," Sean said.

"Where were you earlier?" Quinn asked Gill.

"I was—at home," Gill said.

"Why not work?"

"Ah, hell! I meant to call in; I never did." Gill sounded disgusted with himself. "I knew I was going to help Sean. I just...I was late."

"Didn't matter. You came to help me," Sean said. "And..." He sank down on the steps.

"We just heard," Hattie explained softly to Sean.

"Again, I'm sorry. I'm going to have to ask you to come down to the station with me."

"What?" Gill demanded. "You can't demand anything— and what the hell? I didn't work for that stupid horror place!"

"We need help," Quinn said. "I talked to Chrissy earlier."

"Yeah, I know," Gill said resentfully.

"Thing is, you two were there at Casey's and Sean's before the killing. And you were there again soon after. And you don't have any alibi for those hours right when Abernathy was being killed. I'm sorry; we're going to have to talk. You have to remember something else. You need to remember something else."

"You're not a cop."

"You can take a ride in with me—or I can have a dozen cops out here before you can snap your fingers," Quinn told him.

"I thought you said he was a nice guy?" Gill said, his tone bitter, as he looked at Sean.

"I am a nice guy—doing what's needed."

"You can't think that I killed people!" Gill protested.

"You're not being accused. You're being asked to help," Sean said.

"What about guys who work at the place?" Gill asked.

"Ned Denton, night manager, is down there now, too," Quinn informed him.

Sean was staring at Quinn blankly. "No, no, can't be!" he whispered.

"We just need information," Quinn said.

Gill shook his head. "The girls...Casey and Chrissy. I was going to go and get Chrissy."

"She's still at work?" Quinn asked. It was getting late. Already almost eight, he thought.

"They have to finish their Christmas projects!" Gill said.

"I'll get them. I'll get them both," Sean said. "I'll bring them both to Quinn's."

Gill sighed. "You got a hypnotist or something for me? I don't know anything!"

"We're really hoping that you do," Quinn said

"All right, all right, let me get my stuff."

Sean looked at Quinn, confused, and hurt. "My boss is dead. A guy was killed in my yard. And you're dragging my friend down to the police station?"

"Elimination," Quinn said simply. "And he may know what he doesn't know he knows."

Gill came around, carrying his backpack.

"Ready," he said. "You're not going to cuff me, or anything?"

"Like you said; I'm not a cop."

"Everything will be all right!" Hattie promised. She smiled at Quinn. "Sean, you go get those young ladies. Gill, see if can't somehow help the police. I'm going to lock myself up in my brand new panic room until one of you calls me!"

She turned and headed into her house.

Gill, Sean, and Quinn headed out of the yard. Quinn was glad to see a patrol car parked just down from his own car.

The police would be watching over Hattie's house. Still, he hadn't known about it before now, but he was glad Hattie had a nice new panic room.

Unless, of course, she had just been saying that as a safety precaution.

Sean turned back to stare at the house. "I was...I was almost feeling good!" he said.

Quinn had no answer for that.

"We'll see you back at the house," he told Sean, and he led Gill Martin to his own car.

He wasn't sure what the hell he was doing. He wasn't a cop. But, when he'd been a cop, he'd learned that people often had a lot more to say when they were sitting in an interrogation room—facing an authority that could bring them down, and knew just what questions to ask.

***

"Good is countered by bad; Heaven is countered by Hell, and between the two lie worlds where the dead walk. Dead such as the 'Jack' told about in old Irish tales, for Jack taunted the devil, and thus walks the netherworld. Creatures of Darkness are cast there, as that 'Jack,' working their way not into Heaven, but into Hell, perhaps the devil's spawn, perhaps those who have failed in their promises or vows. Death does not take them as it does others; in their bones like evil, in their ashes, malice and hatred and all that must be fought with light and goodness."

"Okay, okay, so...ashes. Someone dug up ashes and...made them then into something. And whatever that something is, Gretchen Avery had it, somehow got it to Marc Henson. And...."

Danni read again.

"Conquer ash with ash," she read aloud. "Blessed be that which is Holy, goodness that transcends religion; that which is kindness and care, and thus Holy."

She paused, reaching for her phone. She almost jumped out of her chair; it rang as she reached for it.

"Danni."

"Yes?"

"It's Eric. Eric Garfield."

"You found something?"

"Did you?"

"I think someone dug up Marc Henson's ashes. Do you know where he was buried?"

"That's what I just found! Not buried—interred. In the No-name Cemetery."

"The what?"

"It's still on private property. It was a family cemetery from years and years back—never moved. It's not far from me."

"No-name?" Danni repeated. "Eric, I've lived here my whole life. What? St. Louis #1, #2, and #3, and they ran out of names?"

"No, no, it was a family cemetery from before the fires in the late 1700s. It's just a couple of mausoleums in the back of a house that look like sheds or something from the street. Its rental property now, but the owners are still the original family. It's vacant at the moment—the family is remodeling. And they're innocent—been over in Europe the last few months. But, Danni, Marc Henson was buried there. His sister—never a cult member—was the mother of the LaClare family that owns it now. I think that someone tampered with the thing; I'm heading there now."

"Eric, no, not by yourself. Wait!" She started to say, "I'll go with you." She knew that would be a mistake. "I'm calling Quinn; he'll go with you."

"Danni, there have been two murders now. I have to get out there—"

"You need to live. I'm calling Quinn. Don't you dare move!"

She hung up and dialed Quinn. He didn't answer. She swore softly and started to dial Larue, but Quinn was already calling her back.

"Eric knows where Marc Henson was buried—or interred. Quinn, he wants to head right out. He can't head out there alone!"

"Both Ned Denton and Gill Martin are with me. And I really do think it had to be one of them. Or Chrissy. But, Chrissy was at work all day, so she didn't kill Abernathy."

"You're sure she was at work?" Danni asked.

"She was when I went by." He was quiet a minute. "I don't get a read on her. I can't tell if she's really horrified by what's happening...or if she isn't a little slimy."

"I haven't met her, remember, so I can't tell you if I get a feel around her or not."

"I know, Danni. Thing is, this has all moved so fast."

"Yes, but, Casey and Sean seem to think that Gill and Chrissy are their good friends."

"Denton put on a good show when Abernathy's body was found."

"It could be none of them!" Danni said.

She could almost see Quinn shaking his head. "Someone had to have known their house and been to *Horrible Hauntings.*"

"Well, Eric Garfield doesn't really fit that bill. And he wants to go to the mausoleum. Quinn, I don't think he should go alone. I can go; I can take Wolf..."

"No. I'll go. Okay. Like I said, I'm at the police station; I brought Gill Martin in here—Larue already had Denton. I'll leave both sweating it out a little with Larue, run by the house for Wolf, and then I'll head over and get Eric. Let him know I'm coming. Danni, did you get any closer to finding out who might be the killer *now*?"

"Working on it."

"Work fast."

"I will!"

She hung up. The house seemed strangely quiet. Glancing at her watch, she saw that it was almost nine. Billie had probably closed up for the day, or he was doing so now.

She needed to concentrate. Quinn was swinging on by; it would take him a few minutes. If she was lucky, she just might find something that led to their current killer.

Marc Henson, cult leader, had had a sister—presumably not involved. Her family now owns the property where her brother had been interred in their little family cemetery. Marc Henson had been interred in a crypt—a small mausoleum, a little house-like structure that really belonged in one of the "cities of the dead." "A year and a day" was the time given in most interments for a body to decompose enough to be shoveled back into a vault's holding cell so that another body could be interred. Henson had been dead decades. He was surely pure ash and bone.

Who the hell had been on the property?

She needed to speak with Eric—yes! She'd forgotten to tell him that Quinn would be coming for him. And, she needed to know who had been renting the house previously.

Eric answered her quickly.

"Quinn is coming for you. Eric, who does the family use as a realtor?"

"McMichaels and DuMonde," he said. "Why?"

"Going into records," she told him. "Quinn should be there soon."

"All right, all right. I'll wait."

"Thank you."

She hung up and brought out her computer and looked up the realtors. She warned herself she would probably find a number of names that meant nothing.

Finding the records wasn't as easy as she thought; she was sent from one page to the next, and a few pages that led back to the site pages where she had already been.

The door to the office opening broke into her concentration. She almost jumped.

It was Quinn. She smiled. He always seemed impossibly imposing. Very handsome, of course. But imposing—even intimidating—as well.

"Hey!" she said. "You need to get to Eric. I'm afraid he's going to get impatient and leave without you."

"I'm going; I figured we might need Wolf—a little warning if someone was watching or followed us. And, of course, I was checking on you."

"Quinn—I also read something here. 'Conquer ash with ash.' But, it also talks about goodness and holiness." She hesitated. "I think you need to get some of that ash, too, and call Father Ryan and get to him and get him to bless the ash...in case."

"Will do."

She smiled and glanced down at the latest screen to pop on to her computer.

She gasped.

"What? What?" Quinn asked.

She looked up at him. "Quinn, a Gilbert Martin looked at the property where Marc Henson was interred. Gilbert. Gill Martin."

"I'll take Wolf with me; you stay tight. Make sure Billie closes the shop now, okay? And when Sean gets here with Casey and Chrissy—keep them all in the kitchen with the three of you. I'll tell Billie to be prepared for anything. Ned is at the station, but..."

"We'll watch Chrissy like a hawk," she promised.

He turned to leave, then strode for the desk instead. He bowed down and found her lips and kissed her. It was a brief kiss, gentle, passionate...

She smiled. It was somehow incredibly sustaining.

"Take Wolf!" she told him.

"Wolf should be here."

"No—here is safe. You're heading off to an old mausoleum...where people might have been practicing very bad things. Please, Quinn, you worry about me. Let me worry about you. I have Billie and Bo Ray. Please, take Wolf."

"All right, all right, I will. And you...no going away from Billie and Bo Ray."

"I promise."

Then he turned and hurried out.

Danni closed her father's book and headed out as well; she wanted to make sure the shop was closed up tight—and the door was locked between them and Mr. and Mrs. Devil Demon.

She just wasn't sure about the pair.

***

When he left the house on Royal Street, Quinn called Father Ryan, gave him the address, and received his promise to meet him there—with Holy water.

Right after, Quinn paused to call Larue.

"I think Gill Martin might be our killer. I don't know it—but he has no alibi for today, he was at Sean's, knows Sean's, and was hanging around the first murder scene."

"So far, he's not saying anything. He's worried about his girlfriend. My captain is in with him now—I stepped out for a bit. We're doing good cop/bad cop."

"Everyone knows that ploy!" Quinn said.

"Hey, it still works sometimes. Are you coming back in here?"

"I have a project...Seeing Eric Garfield. Then I'll call and see how you're doing, okay?"

"All right. But, if you want me keeping either of these guys..."

"Yes?"

"You need to turn up some evidence."

"I'll be trying," Quinn said.

Eric was waiting for him down by the sidewalk when Quinn arrived.

"Thanks for—for this," Eric said. "I don't know what the hell we're going to find, but, if someone has been tampering with the ashes..."

"No. Thank you," Quinn said, holding the door open for Eric to hop in.

"We're not even going a mile," Eric said. "I could have walked."

"Better that we're together. And I have Wolf."

Wolf barked and wagged his tail. He'd gotten to know Eric, Quin realized.

And he seemed to like him.

Wolf tended to be a pretty good judge of character.

When they arrived at the property, Father Ryan came riding up right behind them.

"A priest?" Eric asked.

"Hey, yeah, fight fire with fire, right?" Quinn said. He didn't know what Eric thought, what he believed, what he suspected, and what he might think of as insane. "Cover all our bases," Quinn added.

They parked in front of the house. It had all the appearances of an abandoned dwelling; chipping paint, overgrown yard, tangles of bushes here and there, and crowds of trees dripping moss.

It wasn't dressed up for Halloween. It had the eerie and spooky quality of a Halloween house without any decoration at all.

The moon had risen, casting a strange glow over the house and yard.

There seemed to be a fog, clinging to the ground and shrubbery, obscuring their vision, promising of something that lurked within.

Father Ryan looked grim.

Eric Garfield kept swallowing.

Quinn quickly introduced the two men. "Well, then, we're after some ashes, eh?" Father Ryan asked.

"Well, we'll see what we see, right? Eric asked. "I've studied the property—on a map. Through there."

He pointed to something of a poor trail around the two-story, colonial-style house.

"Built in the late 1850s," Eric said. "Just before the Civil War. Henson's family had a long history here; he just...just went whacko with the cult and power and..."

"You didn't find anything on a descendent of his?" Quinn asked, pushing his way through the bushes.

"Not yet; he was the last I know about or could find out about any kind of strange axe murders that followed in the wake of the Axeman."

They reached the back of the house. For a moment Quinn turned back and surveyed the eerie, decaying elegance of the old home. Then he turned back to the yard. Though a haze of moss he could see the mausoleums, built to echo the colonial beauty of the house. But, they, too, were decaying.

Eric hurried ahead. He threw his flashlight on a plaque attached to the first. "Interments started in the Civil War...this one...we're up to the 1950s."

Quinn walked around to the second mausoleum. He found a similar plaque and looked at the names. "This one," he said. "It picks up in 1920. But...Henson's name isn't here."

"It wouldn't be there; the family wouldn't have put his name. It would have been an invitation to every would-be cult follower out there. Only someone who knew..." Father Ryan said.

"Of course," Quinn murmured. He walked around the back, where the "holding container" would be.

Someone had broken in the wall there.

Father Ryan came around by his side. He crossed himself. "It's a separate...it's just for Henson. Not even his family wanted their ashes mixed with his. What matters is..."

"Are there any ashes left?" Quinn asked softly.

"Ashes left?" Eric asked.

Wolf suddenly began to whine. Quinn trained his flashlight into the pit within the tomb.

The night seemed to darken; the moon slipped behind a cloud. It caused a pitch-black shadow to sweep over the yard.

"Hurry," Father Ryan said. And while Quinn worked at tearing out more of the wall to find the ash and bits of bone at the bottom of the cell, Father Ryan began a series of prayers in Latin, his words tumbling out.

He handed Quinn a little metal receptacle.

Quinn got down on his knees, scooping out the ash and bits of bone, slipping them into the receptacle.

"What the hell?" Eric muttered.

It seemed that the darkness was slipping over them.

Father Ryan spoke even more quickly.

The darkness began to recede.

"What...oh, Lord!" Eric said. He was breathing heavily; standing there shaking. He stared at Quinn, and then at Father Ryan. Ryan's eyes were closed; he was still speaking softly in Latin.

Father Ryan looked at Quinn. "I believe we're through here."

Quinn nodded. "I want to get back to the shop."

"Of course," Father Ryan said.

They headed out to the cars. As they did so, Quinn's phone rang. It was Larue.

"Hey, my friend, I didn't know if you were coming in or not, but...both Denton and Gill Martin are out of here. Both of them lawyered up. I had nothing."

"Thanks," Quinn said tensely.

"Let's go," he told the others.

He knew it was imperative that he get back to the house on Royal Street.

Chapter 10

"Billie, Bo Ray?" Danni asked.

She looked out the shop windows trying to peer around the various decorations and goods in *The Cheshire Cat*. Something had just made a strange noise in one of the windows. A crinkling noise, or a rustling noise.

Bo Ray had just locked up and headed on into the kitchen to see if Billie had started anything up for dinner. She was alone.

"Hey!" she called.

No one answered her.

"Wolf?" she murmured.

The dog wasn't there; she had made Quinn take him!

Then, as she stood there perplexed, the house was suddenly pitched into complete darkness.

There were no storms about; the wind wasn't blowing. Someone had done something, shut down the circuit breaker...

She had auxiliary lights, set up on an automatic generator, a safety against the storms that did plague the area.

They would go on.

But, for the moment, she was left in absolute darkness.

And she felt strangely as if there was a shadow, even in the darkness, something that began to look over the house on Royal Street like an ebony blanket of pure evil.

The dim floor lights flicked on, a strange, fluorescent green color. And when she looked toward the front of the shop—still so dim and pale, with only the green glow and the light filtering in from the street—she could have sworn that the mannequins had moved.

Mr. and Mrs. Devil Demon. They were looking at her. And their faces had changed. Mrs. Devil Demon wasn't smiling her come-hither smile.

Her mouth was opened in an O of horror.

"Danni!"

She heard her name spoken. It wasn't Billie, and it wasn't Bo Ray. It was a sound like the wind through dry and brittle leaves.

It was a sound like someone...dead.

There was a bang on the window; she jerked around and saw someone outside, someone trying to reach her, to draw her attention. She walked toward the door.

Mr. and Mrs. Devil Demon still seemed to be looking at her. Now, it seemed that they followed her movements, as if they were trying to reach out for her.

The dolls were...almost touching her.

And she saw Natasha was outside, her beautiful face pressed to the glass; she was screaming something.

The door from the shop to the hallway suddenly burst open. She expected to see Billie or Bo Ray, someone who would calm her fear, make her realize the darkness didn't mean that anything had changed.

Someone came into the shop—through the kitchen hallway. And in that dim and pale light, she saw a woman standing there, staring at her.

She was sweating and shaking and dripping with blood.

And held an axe in her hand.

***

Quinn thanked Father Ryan and promised to keep him in the loop on what was happening, and then dropped a very-shaken Eric Garfield back off at his own home.

He got back in his car, but before he could get the automobile in gear, he got a call from Jez, Natasha's assistant.

"We think we've got something," Jez told him. "One of Natasha's friends just stopped in. She said she'd gotten very nervous. Two people had been in her shop asking about black magic. They were playing it cool, trying to pretend they just wanted to jinx a very bad friend who had been cruel to someone. They just wanted to find out where in NOLA they could find a shop with the 'real' thing. She was offended, of course—she's the real deal, a priestess like Natasha. That's why she remembered them."

"Did she tell you anything about these people?" Quinn asked. He wasn't surprised that there were two of them.

If Ned Denton was innocent, that meant Gill Martin and Chrissy Monroe might be...a murderous couple. It had happened before.

But Chrissy had been at work all that day—or had she been there?

"Yes, she said they were both men."

"Thanks, Jez. Where is Natasha?"

"She's gone to see Danni; to tell her. To see if she couldn't figure out something once she knew two men might be involved—and that the Medusa costume might have thrown us all off."

"It did. Thanks, Jez. I'm on my way there now," Quinn told him.

Wolf, sitting in the passenger seat, barked and whined nervously.

Quinn realized then that he, too, felt the need to hurry.

***

"Help me!" the woman whispered, staggering forward.

The axe dropped from her hand to the floor.

Stunned, it took Danni a minute to react. Then she rushed forward, just as the woman started to fall. There was a wound in her head, it seemed, a wound that was causing the blood that dripped down her face and onto the floor.

"Chrissy?" she whispered. She could still hear Natasha banging on the glass windows to the store.

What was going on. Billie...Bo Ray...were they all right?

"Yes, I'm Chrissy and I'm...oh, God, I'm dying! I'm bleeding and dying and..."

"I'll call 911. Hold on, hold on!" Danni said. She had left her cell in the basement! That was all right; the shop had a land line. She eased Chrissy to the floor, looking around for something with which to bind the wound. A dressed up "Gretel" was nearby; she ripped the cotton skirt off the large, collectible doll and wrapped Chrissy's head as best she could.

She rushed over and tried the phone.

It was dead.

No, not dead.

That strange, rustling sound was coming over the line.

A sound that seemed to form her name.

"Danni..."

She slammed the phone down and rushed back to Chrissy, hunkering down by her. "Chrissy, what happened? How did you get in here? Where is Billie...Bo Ray."

"Sean brought me...and then..."

Her eyes closed. She had passed out.

Danni prayed Chrissy had just passed out, that she hadn't died.

Danni didn't want to go back to the hallway; whatever had happened to this woman had happened there, or in the kitchen or studio or out by the garage entrance.

She ran back to the counter, anxious to get the keys to the front door, to get it open, get to Natasha...get help.

Then, the door burst open again.

And she saw a man standing there. He stood there for a moment, staring at her.

And then he smiled, and, of course, she knew.

"Dead, is she?" he asked, as lightly and politely as if he was asking if it was indeed raining.

"Who the hell are you?" Danni demanded.

The axe was still on the floor, right where it had fallen when Chrissy had dropped it.

Far closer to the man than it was to her.

"Son of Satan?" he asked her. "I go back; I am the spirit. I am flesh, but I walk with the devil, with the evil of the ages. I am essence, and I am power."

"You're a bloody murderer, flesh and blood, and you will bleed and die," Danni promised him.

"Ah, the great Danielle Cafferty speaks! No, this is your time, my dear, your time to go."

A weapon, she needed a weapon...

She slipped to the floor, ready to fly for the axe that he most likely had not seen as yet.

But, as she did so...

Black fog arose around her.

For a moment, through that fog, she saw Mr. and Mrs. Devil Demon. They had moved again, coming closer, she thought...

But, they still didn't seem to be evil.

As she moved, desperate to leap for the weapon, she saw the little jack-o-lanterns. The little jack-o-lanterns that had been dropped off by the local artist, hoping that she would sell them on commission.

And she realized...

The darkness, the shadows, and the evil...

All were emitting from the jack-o-lanterns.

***

Quinn knew there was something wrong before he reached Royal Street.

He drove the car into the garage; Wolf leapt past him, almost knocking him back into the car. The dog was in such a hurry to get out.

And then he saw the courtyard was a melee. Bloody bodies lay about; in the first moments, he didn't even know to whom they belonged. He saw Wolf flying at someone who was battling Billie McDougall. For a moment, stunned, the man was down. Then he rose, and picked up Wolf, and threw him across the courtyard.

Quinn had been a cop before he'd been a P.I.

And he acted on instinct.

He swiftly drew his Smith & Wesson 9 mil, aimed—

And fired.

He hit his target, the man going back after Billie McDougall.

Then the man dropped down.

And got right back up. And Quinn saw it was Ned Denton, but a Ned Denton looking nothing like the man he had been before. His face was twisted and warped with rage; his body jerked and moved like that of an automaton.

Bullets were doing nothing to him.

And then, of course, Quinn reached into his pocket, for the blessed ashes of Marc Henson.

He raced forward, heedless of the raging man coming at him.

He drew out some of the ash and threw it at Ned Denton.

The man dead stopped.

He stared at Quinn, that horrible rage still in his eyes.

Along with disbelief.

Then he fell, dead.

Quinn spun around—there were three bodies on the ground. He could discern them all now; Sean DeMille, Casey Cormier, and Bo Ray! He started to kneel down by Casey first, but, Billie rushed over, shouting.

"Quinn, Quinn, get into the house! The second one...Gill. Gill Martin, he's gone after his girl, Chrissy...and Danni's in there!"

At that same moment, Natasha came running around to the courtyard, panting and in a sheer panic.

"The shop, Quinn! He's in the shop!"

Quinn didn't need another word. He tore on into the house, so dimly lit now in an eerie green glow from their auxiliary lights.

***

"I have come," the man said. "To bring you to hell!"

Danni tried to move; she felt as if she was submerged in the dark fog, as if her limbs couldn't move. She could only watch as the man came forward, smiling.

Just staring at her. Smiling that smile. Dropping down to kick Chrissy's arm aside, and pick up the axe.

She couldn't move; she absolutely couldn't move. She tried, and it was like trying to swim through a tar field.

The axe was coming, but...

There was suddenly something between her and the man.

The mannequins. Mr. Devil Demon, there, the other behind him, trying to block the man who was coming, so determined.

He laughed, and slammed Mr. Devil Demon out of the way.

He raised the axe...

But, Mrs. Devil Demon was there.

He threw his arm out, sending her hurling over a barrel with a display containing a scarecrow and corncobs, and tiny Styrofoam tombstones.

He was facing Danni.

And she could just...stare.

Then suddenly, she heard the sound of a gun firing.

The man's eyes widened, and he staggered back.

But, then he smiled, and just kept coming forward again.

"Danni!" Quinn shouted.

"No, careful, the fog...it will paralyze you!" she warned, her voice as thick as the shadow; she could hardly move her lip, hardly make sound.

Then something seemed to fly through the air like confetti.

Ashes and tiny bits of bone and more ashes...

And to Danni's vast relief; he stopped. He stared at her.

And he wasn't smiling. His eyes were purely incredulous— and filled with a fire and fury.

"Evil will live forever! For I am spirit!"

"You are flesh and blood!" Danni said. "And we'll burn every one of these wretched little jack-o-lanterns with the ashes of the past, and this evil will die forever."

He let out a scream unlike anything she had ever heard before. A scream that seemed to rip from the bowels of Hell, as if all the souls in damnation had risen to cry out as well.

And then he dropped, flat to the ground, his eyes open.

He was dead.

Quinn stepped over the fallen "Devil Demon" dolls, hurrying toward her. But she was behind the counter; there, with the cute little jack-o-lanterns, dropped off by...a woman.

And evil beyond comprehension.

"Quinn, the jack-o-lanterns!"

"The jack-o-lanterns?"

"Yes, do you have..."

"Ash!" he said.

And there, on the old mahogany bar turned into a sales counter, he doused the jack-o-lanterns in the ash he still had from the little metal receptacle he carried.

A scream echoed on the air, no real voice, just a rustle...

Like dry leaves.

Then the fog was gone.

And the darkness was gone.

And the lights came back up.

Danni and Quinn ran into one another's arms. And for long, long moments, they simply held one another.

And those moments were very beautiful, and very good.

Epilogue

Largely thanks to Natasha, no one at the house on Royal Street, in the courtyard or in the street—other than the bad guys!—died that night.

By the time Billie had started trying to tend to the others, Natasha had already called the police and the paramedics.

Neither Gill Martin nor Ned Denton had managed to get a good aim at anyone with the one axe they had procured before coming over.

Sean DeMille had taken a good swing to his side, but, while he'd bled a lot, his wounds had been superficial. The axe blade had sheered the side of Bo Ray's head; he told them all that it was a damned good thing he'd been hard-headed. Casey had been slammed down on the ground—left for later, once Billie McDougall had been taken out.

Apparently, Sean had picked Casey and Chrissy up from work; then Gill had come on over and Chrissy had opened the door for him. Ned Denton had been with him.

And all hell had broken out.

It was two days later; Halloween was just around the corner. Chrissy was in the hospital still—where she would be for some time, Quinn thought. She wasn't only going to need medical care; she would need some serious therapy.

He had suspected her. He had thought maybe she'd been jealous of Casey's work, and thus, Casey had become a victim to tease with another victim—her murder planned for later.

"It's hard to ken, hard to ken," Billie said.

They were sitting around the dining room table. Their group—Father Ryan, Natasha, Jez, Billie, Bo Ray, Danni, and himself—and Sean DeMille and Casey Cormier.

Sean and Casey had talked about leaving the second they were out of the hospital, but Danni had insisted that they not.

Halloween could still be a good holiday. There were children counting on Sean. And Hattie had been so kind.

And, so, they were just finishing up dinner—half of their group well-bandaged and filled with aspirin—getting ready to head over for a special viewing of Hattie's yard and Sean's open house. They had a few minutes and lingered over coffee.

"This is what we discovered," Danni explained. "There was a man who the police had actually suspected of the axe murders years ago. His descendent was Gretchen Avery, and she knew to find her father's ashes and use evil to awaken them. The cult leader—Marc Henson—was one of her children, but he had gone away and changed his name. His family was horrified by him—and hid his name when they interred him. Anyway, it turns out that Gill Martin discovered he was a grandchild of Gretchen Avery, and he followed the trail to Marc Henson—and finally found the right spell at a shop somewhere in New Orleans—and dug up Marc Henson's ashes. What caused the damage was the jack-o-lanterns."

"I could have sworn it was a woman who brought them in!" Bo Ray moaned.

"And I thought Medusa was a woman!" Jez reminded him.

"It was never Chrissy," Quinn said.

"Never Chrissy," Danni agreed.

"Well, my jack-o-lantern and all the jack-o-lanterns you had have been destroyed along with the blessed ash," Casey said. "But, how do we know..."

"That there aren't more out there?" Quinn asked. "There may be. But, without the flesh and blood men alive who awoke the evil, they really haven't any power. We'll try to find them, of course, if there are more. But, they will be powerless now. Even if they were paper mache—mixed with ashes."

"How did the two get together?" Sean asked. "I thought Ned was a great guy. I thought Gill was our friend."

"Poor Chrissy. She'll never get over this," Casey said.

"I'll be seeing to her," Father Ryan promised.

"The two didn't even meet at your house, Sean, so you weren't to blame—you were just used. You were Gill's friend and Ned's work associate. Apparently, well, Natasha?"

"They met at a black-market shop somewhere in the city; Larue is on that. He'll be looking into getting it closed down— they have all kinds of horrible animal sacrifices and sell hardcore drugs, according to my very scared source," Natasha said. "And they discovered they both knew you, Sean, through Chrissy, and thought your house would be a wonderful way to begin. They did intend a mass murder somewhere on Halloween. They thought they needed to rid the world of Quinn and Danni first, and if they got to Danni—well, Quinn would walk into a trap."

"It's amazing!" Sean whispered. "That such evil can exist!"

Wolf, still nursing an injured paw, woofed, as if in total agreement.

"Ah, yes, but it's equally amazing that the good to counter it exists as well!" Danni said softly, and she stood. "Hey! Kids are coming. Let's get over to Hattie's."

They left—locking up carefully—and walked down to Esplanade. Hattie was already there, waiting in the yard with Detective Jake Larue. He was off-duty, but being Larue, he wanted to see to this.

He didn't want to know how they'd brought down Denton and Martin; he was just glad they had.

And he was smiling as he came toward them.

Quinn watched Danni greet Hattie and Larue, and then walk up to the mannequins—Mr. and Mrs. Devil Demon.

She'd seen to it they were completely repaired.

She kissed each on the cheek, smiling, and then stepped back, slipping into his arms.

"You just kissed mannequins," he told her.

She smiled, shaking her head. "I just kissed some kind of goodness," she told him. "I don't understand how or why, but they are imbued with...love and care and protection." She looked up at him. "It is a mystery I will pursue!"

He smoothed her hair back. Dear God, but he was in love with her.

A bus drove up to empty out a load of excited children.

"Oh, watch them as they go in! They're adorable!" Danni said.

"We could have a few of our own," he told her.

"We could. We could really do that marriage thing first."

"Yes, we do need to do that, but...hm."

"Yes?"

"While we're in the planning stages, don't they say something about practice?"

"Kids here!" she whispered.

"I'm being totally PG!"

She watched as the kids screamed delightedly as Sean's giant dinosaur seemed to do a bow.

Then she turned in his arms and told him.

"So...later. You don't have to be PG."

"I don't intend to be," he promised her. And as she smiled up at him, he said, "I'm going straight for an X-rating."

She laughed, and they watched the children.

Laughing, shrieking, having so much fun.

And, he decided, Halloween was one of those holidays you had to watch out for.

But, it could also be pretty great as well.

New York Times and USA Today best-selling author Heather Graham majored in theater arts at the University of South Florida. After a stint of several years in dinner theater, back-up vocals, and bartending, she stayed home after the birth of her third child and began to write, working on short horror stories and romances. After some trial and error, she sold her first book, WHEN NEXT WE LOVE, in 1982 and since then, she has written over two hundred novels and novellas including category, romantic suspense, historical romance, vampire fiction, time travel, occult, and Christmas holiday fare. She wrote the launch books for the Dell's Ecstasy Supreme line, Silhouette's Shadows, and for Harlequin's mainstream fiction imprint, Mira Books.

Heather was a founding member of the Florida Romance Writers chapter of RWA and, since 1999, has hosted the Romantic Times Vampire Ball, with all revenues going directly to children's charity. She is pleased to have been published in approximately twenty languages, and to have been honored with awards from Waldenbooks. B. Dalton, Georgia Romance Writers, Affaire de Coeur, Romantic Times, and more. She has had books selected for the Doubleday Book Club and the Literary Guild, and has been quoted, interviewed, or featured in such publications as The Nation, Redbook, People, and USA Today and appeared on many newscasts including local television and Entertainment Tonight.

Heather loves travel and anything having to do with the water, and is a certified scuba diver. Married since high school graduation, and the mother of five, her greatest love in life remains her family, but she also believes her career has been an incredible gift, and she is grateful every day to be doing something that she loves so very much for a living.

Made in the USA
Middletown, DE
04 September 2020

17825283R00076